THUNDER IN THE SKY

K. M. Peyton

ILLUSTRATED BY VICTOR AMBRUS

RED FOX

A RED FOX BOOK

Published by Arrow Books Limited
20 Vauxhall Bridge Road, London SW1V 2SA

An imprint of the Random Century Group

London Melbourne Sydney Auckland Johannesburg
and agencies throughout the world

First published in Great Britain in 1966
by Oxford University Press
Re-issued by The Bodley Head 1985
Red Fox edition 1990

Text © K. M. Peyton 1966

Printed and bound in Great Britain by
Courier International Ltd, Tiptree, Essex

ISBN 0 09 975150 X

To Jonathan

1 A New Skipper

Gil and Sam Goodchild sat on the wall in the warm September sunshine, looking across the making tide to the fleet of barges lying up against Meeson's mill. They sat in silence, unusually solemn-faced, listening to the whirr of the reapers in the fields all round them, the clop of hooves over the bridge, the cry of a drifting gull above the topmasts. It was all utterly familiar and unremarkable, and yet today, and after today, nothing was going to be the same again.

Two men were coming towards them over the bridge.

They carried kit-bags on their shoulders and were waving back at the men on the barges. Gil and Sam slipped off the wall and went to meet them.

Sam said, ' We were waiting to say good-bye.'

' Aye, lad. Well, look after the old girl. Fair winds and all that. I hope your new skipper'll be as easy on you as I was.'

' Yes, and I hope your new skipper'll be easy on you too,' Sam said, and they all laughed.

' You cheek him like you cheeked me and he'll belt you, that's for sure,' the man said. The two skippers were leaving the barges to join the army, and the boys could sense their half-excitement, half-uncertainty, as they stood for the last time by the tide which no longer concerned them. They all shook hands. Gil mumbled shyly, colouring up, and one of the men said, ' You teach that young brother of yours to mind his tongue, Gil. By the time I come back he'll have learnt some sense, I dare say.'

' What, by Christmas? ' the other man said, and they laughed again.

' I hope it lasts long enough for me to go,' Sam said, not joking, but earnest.

' Not a chance, mate. You're only fifteen. You'll only be fifteen when we're back. Cheerio, then. Our train'll be along in a minute.'

' Good-bye. Good luck.'

The two skippers went on up the hill towards the station that sat perched among cornfields on the single-line track that followed the river down to Burnham, and the two boys who had been their respective mates on board the barges *Trilby* and *Flower of Ipswich* turned back to the river to watch the rest of the barges making ready to go. *Trilby* and the *Flower* had to wait until two new skippers arrived, and their mates had to wait with them.

' Seems queer,' Gil said.

Sam agreed. He was thinking if he had been Gil, he

would be on his way up the hill to the station too, not
waiting about for an old barge to sail. Gil was seventeen,
old enough to join up if he had wanted to. Manny, their
elder brother who had been skipper of *Ethel Mary*, had
volunteered a month ago. But Gil had never spoken about
it. Queer, Sam thought. But Gil had meant queer the
barges sailing without them. Perhaps, even, queer to think
there was a war on. The whirring of the reapers like the
whirring of giant crickets gave no hint that anything
was different this year from last. The little village of Battlesbridge slumbered in the heat, and there was scarcely breeze
enough to stir a sail. Sam could feel the dust of the cornfields
on his face and the sweat between his shoulder-blades. It was
the September of 1914, and the summer had been exception-
ally hot. To work on barges had been more pleasure than
work, even if the passages had been slow in the light breezes
and the pay consequently the poorer.

The tide was full now, and the first topsail was breaking
out against the towering brick walls of the flour mill.
Deep-loaded with flour, the barges were bound for London,
the *Thomas and Anne*, *Good Intent*, *Martha* and *Paglesham*.

The mate on the *Good Intent*, a friend of Sam's, heaved in
the mooring warp. Sam cast off for him, and said, ' You
heard who your new skipper's going to be yet? '

Sam shook his head.

The boy said, ' Old Bunyard wants a boat, since *Emma*
was smashed up in that collision. You might get him.'

Sam made a face. ' I'll soon see.'

' I don't envy you, if it's him. He's a real driver.'

' He can't be worse than your old man,' Sam muttered.

The water widened as the barge slipped away from the
wharf, its topsail filling above the bridge.

' Bunyard's a killer,' Sam's friend shouted.

Sam made a rude gesture after him. Gil was laughing,
throwing stones for the little mongrel, Scruff, that lived on

the barge with him. Sam said, ' What's funny? You might
get Bunyard, come to that.'

' I'm not worried,' Gil said.

Gil had been in barges since he was fourteen, and knew
enough now not to worry overmuch about who was his
boss. He knew his job and his place, and how to avoid
trouble, which Sam with his impetuous temperament and
ready tongue had yet to learn. The barges, for all their size,
were manned by only a skipper and a mate; they plied
round the coast between Yarmouth and London, carrying
anything from stones for roads to hay for the London horse
traffic. It was an independent life, and its rigours quickly
showed up a man's short-comings. Sam did not want to be
found wanting by a man with Bunyard's reputation. His old
skipper, now aboard the train and heading for the training
depot, had been an easy man, and Sam had got used to his
banter and slack ways. Even when Sam had made mistakes,
the old man had only grumbled for a minute or two, no
more. He had never cursed or roared, nor hit him a clip over
the ear, which was the common lot of boys Sam's age. Gil
was all right. At seventeen he was as brawny as any skipper
he was likely to get. But Sam was still growing, a wiry boy,
all wrists and ankles, with an open cheerful face and a grin
which showed a front tooth broken by a blow from a
swinging block. (' Lucky it was only your tooth and not
your brains,' his skipper had remarked happily.) Like all the
Goodchild brothers, he had sandy-red hair, thick and curling;
his eyes were blue-grey, wide-set above the freckle-scattered
cheeks. The sailormen—the bargemen were always called
the sailormen—knew Sam as the cheeky Goodchild; Gil was
the quiet one. Manny had been the solid one, a competent
level-headed skipper of twenty-four who had enlisted the
same week war was declared. To Sam, Manny was more
father than brother. His going had sobered Sam considerably.

They watched the barges depart on the top of the tide. The

enormous tanned brown sails blossomed above the quiet river like a phenomenon of nature. The wind, such as it was, was from the west, fair for the passage down to the sea. The great black hulls, fully loaded, showed only a foot or two above water. On the wide flare of their transoms the sun picked out the gleam of giltwork where the names and ports of register were inscribed; blue scrollwork surrounded the titles, and gold curlicues to either side added a touch of extravagance to the otherwise strictly workmanlike ships. Without them the wharf suddenly looked large and bare, and Sam had a feeling that *Trilby* and the *Flower*, loaded and moored up opposite the mill, were wondering why they weren't going too.

'Waste of a tide,' Sam said. When the tide went out at Battlesbridge there was no water in the river-bed at all, and a barge took the ground. The coming and going of barges was governed entirely by the tide, which meant that they sailed when the tide served, at any hour of the day or night, not tidily at the start of a working day. The next high water at Battlesbridge was at two in the morning, and Sam knew that if the new skippers had arrived by then, that is when they would sail.

'You think they'll come tonight?' he said.

'I should think so,' Gil said. 'It's money wasting, hanging around here. The Guv'nor knows that as well as anyone.'

'Might as well have a sleep then,' Sam said. 'While we've got the chance.'

'I'm going over to see Agnes,' Gil said. 'We might not be up here again for a while.'

'Oh, you . . .' Sam grinned derisively at his brother who had turned his back on the water and started to walk up towards the bridge, Scruff at his heels.

'Stupid girls,' Sam muttered.

It was too good a day to sleep in the dark forepeak of the *Flower of Essex*. Sam walked a little way along the river,

climbed over the sea-wall and dropped down into the red
stubble of a shaved wheatfield. The reapers had passed on
and the field was deserted. Sam made himself a mattress of
four stooks of corn in the shade of the hedge and flung
himself down contentedly. What was it about Agnes, he
wondered, that compelled Gil to hire a bicycle for sixpence
and cycle all the way to Fambridge, a distance of seven or
eight miles, in this sweating heat, when he might be dozing
comfortably in a cornfield? She was only a girl, with two
arms, two legs, a skinny torso and a round bun face. She had
spots and frizzy hair and a voice like a bullfrog's. At school
she had once locked Sam in a cupboard for calling her Fatty.
If Gil was going to start courting, he would be in for a hard
time, for *Trilby* did not come up the Crouch often; this was
only the third time in the last six months. Agnes lived in a
cottage near their own home, but they were rarely at home
now, only if there were no freights, or the barge happened
to be in the neighbourhood. Their mother was used to their
odd comings and goings, for their father had been on the
barges too, until he had fallen down a hatch and been
killed in Ipswich five years ago.

Lying back in the pricking straw, Sam shut his eyes. He
could feel the sweat damp on his thighs under his black serge
trousers and the heavy, dusty smell of summer tickled his
nose. He expected to be asleep within ten minutes, but somehow his mind was restless—worried, almost. He had this
feeling again, that he had had when they had said good-bye
to the two skippers on the bridge, that today his life was
changing, and that this long, hot summer would not happen
again. He turned over, to ease a pricking on his neck, and
said to himself irritably, ' Of course the summer will happen
again, you fool,' but something in his mind insisted that with
his old skipper going, his old easy life was going too, and
the cloudless summer was, in his mind, a part of the easy
life he had got used to.

'It's the war,' he thought. It had touched him twice now, first with Manny going, and now his skipper. And although Manny was Sam's own brother, his going had made no actual change in Sam's life, but the skipper's going had started these unaccountable twinges.

'You're frightened you're going to get Bunyard,' Sam told himself contemptuously.

Was it only that? Sam did not know. He wasn't used to asking himself questions about things that had no answers. He wasn't used to thinking at all, he could almost hear his old skipper saying.

'If it's Bunyard then . . .' Sam tried to think what frightened him about Bunyard. He knew he was one of the old-school sailormen who had served his time in a square-rigger round the Horn before even Sam's own father had been born; he was built like a bull and it was said he never went to sleep. He was a driver, and never hung around wasting a tide if it looked like a blow; he had a reputation for making fast passages and faster turn-rounds.

'But what's wrong with that?' Sam thought. 'I'm not afraid of work, and it'll mean more money.' Besides, it was only Curley Tompkins on *Good Intent* who had brought up the name Bunyard. Just for a lark. 'I'll give him Bunyard,' Sam muttered into the straw. 'I'm not staying awake for anything Curley Tompkins says.'

He slept.

The ebbing tide left the wharf, and *Trilby* and the *Flower of Ipswich* settled heavily on the gravel, where past generations of flat bottoms similarly settling had ironed out hard plateaux on the creek bed. The coloured bobs of the carrying firm that owned them hung limply from the tops of their masts against the shimmering sky, and down the river the barges bound for London drifted with the tide, and the skippers cursed the dying breeze. When Sam awoke it was going dusk. The sky was violet and deep blue, so flawless that Sam had this foreboding again, as soon as he opened his eyes and saw it, that something was in store for him. Faint, green stars flicked the brow of the hill above him. He thought of the war, but it meant nothing to him, save that he was having a new skipper. He got up stiffly, brushed the straw and dust off him, and walked back to the barge along the side of the empty river.

' I bet the others haven't got far,' he thought.

He went on board *Flower* and dropped down into the skipper's quarters to find himself something to eat. Without the skipper's gear lying around, the cramped quarters looked strangely bare and uninviting. Even when he had lit the lamp and the moths were burring in the hatchway and the small table was set with the bread and cheese and jug of milk that he had bought fresh in the village that morning, it was an empty cabin, waiting for a skipper. The stove had gone out and the ashes were spewed on the floor. Sam gave the lamp a perfunctory polish with an old rag, swept up the floor and then relit the fire in case the skipper arrived hungry.

' There's nowt here he can complain about,' he thought, looking round at the glow of varnished panels in the light. He went up on deck and surveyed the hatches all battened down, sheets and halyards neatly coiled, the decks swabbed clean of spilt grain. She was all ready to go, to feel her way on the tide between the winding upper reaches of the Crouch.

' There's a bit of a moon. A drop more wind and we'll do,' Sam thought.

' All we want is a skipper, *Flower*,' he said, touching the spokes of her wheel. The cabin light shone out of the skylight on the top of the hatch; the compass stood in its binnacle, its needle pointing towards the railway line that would bring the missing sailorman down from London. ' They should've promoted me,' Sam thought, leaning on the wheel, looking up at the lacework of shrouds against the stars. He fancied himself as a skipper. ' I'd do you,' he said to the barge.

'I could take you to London, no trouble.' But it would be a few years, five at least, before he got his own barge. And by then, with any luck, he'd have been to war and back. 'This time next year,' he thought, 'I could join the army.' A whole year, but everyone laughed at the thought that the war would still be on in a year's time. Everyone said it would be over by Christmas. How strange Gil was not to go! And yet, somehow, Sam could not see Gil making a very good soldier, not like Manny (nor himself, of course). Gil had always been the quiet one. He liked animals and flowers, and he would stand at the shrouds sometimes, just looking at the sea as if he were thinking about it, in his strange quiet way. Sam thought you probably needed more dash (like himself) to be a good soldier. Gil didn't have dash. He had been the brainiest of the three of them at school, but Sam didn't think that would help a great deal in the making of a soldier. A good soldier, after all, did as his officer told him. What he needed was dash and courage. Sam reckoned he had dash and hoped he had courage.

'*Flower of Ipswich!*'

Sam nearly jumped out of his skin. The voice was like the roar of a wild bull. He started up from the wheel and stared across towards the tow-path. A small kit-bag, packed hard as a bullet, flew past his ear and landed with a thud on deck. Almost immediately a large man swung across by the shrouds. The shape of him in the darkness was almost square, his shoulders the widest Sam had ever seen. But under his cap his hair gleamed white.

'My name's Bunyard,' he said. 'You're the mate, I take it?'

'Yes, sir.' Sam's voice almost quavered. He felt his heart plummet like a shot bird. He stared at the great shape in the darkness. Dash and courage . . . the words faltered through his head. Standing, tongue-tied, before his new skipper, he knew that at that moment he had neither.

2 A Freight for Calais

Bunyard, after a check round his new barge to see all was in order, bore Sam ashore to 'The Barge', a less mobile edifice than her namesakes on the water, to 'have a look at him in a good light'. By the time he had arrived in the crowded little tap-room of the alehouse, Sam had got his wits back and, with native resilience, accepted his fate. Bunyard it was. With a pint of ale on the table before him, he examined Bunyard with as much interest as Bunyard examined him.

Bunyard's eyes, needling him under bushy white eyebrows, were faded blue, very used-looking, Sam thought, and very direct. His face was red and wrinkled, with crimson broken veins flecking the cheeks, and a large nose jutting out in a way that Sam could see could make a reputation for a man. It was a splendid, dominating nose. The mouth below it was hidden by a thick, drooping, yellowish moustache, the jaw jutting and stubborn beneath. Sam did not think he would ever argue with his new skipper. Bunyard, for his part, shook his head over Sam.

' You're just a lad. Fifteen? Sixteen? '

' Sixteen,' Sam lied brazenly.

' God save us,' said Bunyard. He pushed his cap back on his head and scratched his white hair. ' Maybe the Guv'nor will give me a swop.'

Sam felt the temper rise up in him like the froth on his tankard. ' My old skipper never complained,' he said hotly. ' I've been on the *Flower* for a year.'

' Creek-hopping,' said Bunyard. ' Our next freight is for France.'

Sam's eyes widened. ' France! ' After the first shock, a tingling determination seized him. Swop him indeed! ' There's nothing about crossing the Channel any worse than the run down from Yarmouth,' he said fiercely. ' That was our last trip. That's not creek-hopping.'

Bunyard laughed. ' Proper little fox, that's what you are. What do you think of my new mate, Harry? ' He turned to the man sitting at the bench next to him, obviously a sailorman. Sam presumed he was *Trilby's* new master. He looked a milder character altogether than Bunyard, and Sam envied Gil his luck. Harry was looking at Bunyard's problem with an amused expression.

' Better than nothing,' he said. ' Boy or not. I don't seem to have a mate at all.'

' Yes, you have,' Sam said. ' You've got my brother—'

Bunyard gave a great guffaw and nudged Harry in the ribs.

'God help you! You've got his brother. D'you hear that? You've got his brother. His young brother, I bet you.'

'He's older,' Sam muttered angrily. 'And my eldest brother was skipper of *Ethel Mary* before he volunteered.' He wanted to add, 'And he never smashed his barge in any collision,' but did not dare.

'Manny Goodchild?' Bunyard said. 'You're a brother of Manny's?'

'Yes.'

Bunyard grinned. 'I'll take you on that,' he said. 'Manny was a fine skipper. So he volunteered, eh?'

'Yes.'

'Hmm.' Bunyard grunted. 'We'll pick up a third hand at Beckton, if there's anyone without a job. The sailormen will all be grand-daddies like me, and infants like you, come Christmas.'

Barges that went down-Channel always carried a crew of three. Mention of a third hand didn't surprise Sam; he was too busy congratulating himself on having claimed Manny as a close relation.

'I knew your father,' Bunyard told him. 'You're like him, all that red hair and cheek. Your grandfather was on the *Serica* when I was on the *Ariel*.' He heaved a gusty sigh. 'Listen to me, Harry! I'm getting old. Sailing with Isaac Goodchild's grandson for mate . . . and Isaac was younger than me.'

Sam looked at Bunyard dubiously. Bunyard caught his glance and laughed again. He had interpreted it accurately. 'Don't you be thinking I'm past it, young Goodchild. The Goodchilds bred young all down the line. I'm good for years yet.'

This made Sam think of Gil and his interest in Agnes. He looked at *Trilby's* new skipper, and thought Gil would have no trouble with him. He looked about forty, and was as lean as Bunyard was broad. He seemed quiet, but had sharp eyes. He was talking to two young men who were describing in graphic detail the mining of the cruiser *Amphion*.

Interested as he was in his new skipper, Sam could not help his attention straying to this fascinating subject, which had been much discussed amongst the sailormen. The *Amphion* had been sunk by a mine off the Suffolk coast only a few days after the declaration of war, and over a hundred and fifty of her men had been killed. To the coasting traffic the news had come as an abrupt, almost incredible, warning of the reality of the war. Sam, having been less than fifty miles away at the time of the event, had been more impressed by the disaster than by anything since his father's death; Manny had joined up two days later.

'Went up like a ruddy volcano,' one of the men was saying. 'One minute we were steaming along as nice as you like—early morning it was, about half-past six—the next minute, whomp!' He banged an excited fist on the table. 'The whole lot went up in a sheet of flame. The poor beggars up in the bows didn't stand a chance. The explosion up there blew them to bits. And in twenty minutes the ship had gone down.'

The other man, who had burn scars on his face, said, 'The devilish thing about it—there wasn't a Hun in sight. We'd hit one of the ruddy mines the German ship had dropped the day before. We'd sunk her—we'd even got half her survivors on board—then bang! Twenty-four hours later you can say she sank us—that's the ruddy twist.'

The two men, on survivors' leave after the incident, had a good audience for their story in the crowded bar parlour, and there was plenty of beer and sympathy for their experiences. Sam hung over the table, the hot indignation shining in his face.

'Being sunk in fair fight is one thing,' somebody was

saying, 'but being sunk by a dirty trick like that—them ruddy mines are illegal.'

'That's true. They're against the rules of war. You trust the Huns to think up a swindle like that.'

'What's to stop a merchant vessel catching it, or even a neutral, come to that? The Government ought to do something about it.'

'They should lay some of their own. Soon will, I dare say.' Bunyard's quiet comment stopped the rabble of disapproval in its tracks. Several angry faces turned in his direction.

'You believe in the Hun tactics then?' someone said coldly.

'I believe in calling a ruddy spade a spade. What difference does it make if a ship is sunk by a mine or a gun? The effect's the same. If you're talking of dirty tricks, the whole war is one big dirty trick.'

Bunyard's heresy evoked a marked hostility over the tankards. The faces that had shone with righteous indignation clouded with anger. Sam shifted uneasily in his seat beside his new skipper, who seemed not to sense any unwisdom in his remarks. Bunyard took a long draught from his pint, and wiped his big moustache.

'If it's a dirty trick then, you mean these young men aren't fighting for the honour of their country? You mean they're just part of a dirty trick?' a man asked.

'Young men'll always go to war. They go for the sheer hell of it. You can call it patriotism or honour or what you like. But honour doesn't win wars. It's cunning and brute force that wins wars. That's what we want, not claptrap about honour.'

'We've got right on our side! Our men aren't brutes like the Huns that massacred the Belgian women and children! Or are you saying they are?' the man said, glaring at Bunyard.

'There are brutes of all nationalities,' Bunyard said calmly. 'I've sailed with many a German I'd be glad to have for a brother.'

'Whose side are you on, mate?' the sailor growled, his eyes flickering angrily in his burned face.

'The winning side, I hope,' Bunyard said.

'He's a ruddy Hun himself, if he wants a German for a brother,' an inebriated farm labourer shouted.

Bunyard laughed. Someone knocked his beer off the table,

Bunyard stood up like a walrus surfacing, and the next moment there were chairs flying, pints of beer cascading on the floor and fists shooting out in all directions. Sam, practised in such situations, slipped neatly under the table and made a rapid, ducking dash for the door. He felt no conscience at all in not staying to defend his new master, whose opinions, he felt, had brought him merely what he deserved. For an elderly man, though, Sam had to admit the skipper was not making heavy weather of the fracas. A glance behind showed him Bunyard standing calmly against the wall, fending off all comers with an arm like a thick boiled ham. Like all pub fights, the initial cause was rapidly forgotten in the excitement and Sam saw that the sailor with the burns was happily hammering the farm labourer who had joined him in taunting Bunyard. Bunyard, in fact, was shortly able to walk out of the door, unnoticed in the mêlée. He had a pint in his hand, a lone survivor of the upheaval, and sat down calmly on the bench outside.

'What time did the tide turn today?' he asked Sam.

Sam looked at him sideways, cautiously.

'Just after one.'

Bunyard took out a large gold watch at his waist and looked at it. Sam watched him closely. He half-admired the old man for his behaviour, but was shaken by his opinions. Nobody said things like he'd said about Germans. Not in public. Inside the bar the landlord was restoring order. Several of his late customers emerged somewhat precipitously, and disappeared, arguing, into the night. Bunyard sat on, drinking his pint, unmoved. The other skipper came out shortly and joined him, and they started talking shop about their next freight. Sam listened, disturbed by the evening's brief excitement, his slate-coloured eyes slightly glazed by drink and anxiety. His introduction to his new skipper had been rather more than he had bargained for.

Gil came into the yard just before the alehouse closed at

midnight. He saw Sam and stopped by the bench, the little dog at his heels.

'See Agnes?' Sam asked him.

Gil nodded and smiled. His eyes went inquiringly to the two strangers.

'This is my brother Gil,' Sam said to Harry. 'He's mate on *Trilby*.'

The two men looked at each other steadily.

'Harry Finch,' said Harry.

'Pleased to meet you,' said Gil, very politely.

He fetched himself a pint and came back and sat by Sam. The two skippers were talking and Gil grinned at Sam and said softly, 'You got yourself Bunyard then?'

'Looks like it.'

Gil laughed. He seemed in a very cheerful mood.

'How's Agnes then?'

Gil took a long pull at his drink. 'Lovely,' he said.

The inn closed and they went back to the barges. Sam felt worried and careless, because of the beer, but knew from experience that getting the barge under way would quickly sober him up. He followed Bunyard down the tow-path. Gil and Finch were behind him.

Sam heard Finch say, 'What's that ruddy dog doing on board?' His voice was rough and angry.

'That's my dog,' Gil said. 'He lives on board.'

'Not when I'm skipper he doesn't.'

Sam stopped in his tracks, surprised at the tone of Finch's voice. He turned round and saw Gil standing by *Trilby*'s shrouds, one foot on the bulwarks.

'He comes, or neither of us comes,' Gil said. Sam had never heard him sound so cool. Finch growled something and Sam heard Gil say, 'This dog belonged to my brother. He gave him to me to look after when he volunteered.'

There was a pause, and Finch growled something more.

Gil moved forward along the deck and Sam hurried after Bunyard, who was chuckling:

'You Goodchilds! What've we got on board? Pair of tame rabbits?'

'That dog goes everywhere with Gil. It's never lived anywhere but on a barge,' Sam said.

Sam supposed Finch had given way, for Gil was already going about his business to get the barge under way. Bunyard had stopped chuckling and was pulling a frayed smock over his head. The night was cool and clear, a soft westerly blowing round the topmast.

'Come on, lad. Get those stern-warps inboard,' Bunyard said. His voice was sharp. Sam started work.

Flower of Ipswich made a slow passage in light winds into the Thames and laid on the buoys off Woolwich alongside the barges that had left Battlesbridge a tide before her. Bunyard went up to the city to call at the office and see the Guv'nor (who owned the barge) and arrange for the third hand he wanted, and Sam was left with ample opportunity to brag to Curley Tompkins about his next freight.

'Give me a go-ahead skipper like Bunyard any time,' he boasted. 'None of your turnip trade for him. We're loading coke at Beckton tomorrow—for Calais.'

Curley was visibly impressed.

'Go on!'

'Calais? Huh, you'll have to do the old drill with the naval patrol then,' put in Percy Wright, mate of the *Thomas and Anne*. 'They wait for you off Deal, and tell you when you can sail and when you can't. They don't know a thing about barges. If you've got a fair wind and a making tide, they tell you to drop your hook, sure as fate.'

'It's the minefields,' Curley said. 'They tell you how to miss them.'

Sam looked at Curley doubtfully. 'Barge'll go over a
mine,' he said with more conviction than he felt.

'Don't you believe it,' Curley said. 'Another thing, the
Customs'll be all over you like fleas when you get back.
And the old spy-hunters.'

'What old spy-hunters?'

'The police. We had the police down here last night,
before you got in. Old Charlie on the gate says they're

looking for spies. Anyone on a regular run to France they think is a spy. Charlie says so.'

' But nobody *would*—'

' Wouldn't they just? ' said Percy derisively. ' People'll do anything for money. There's not much risk. You take a bit of information across that somebody gives you. Somebody over there's waiting to take it off you. It's easy.'

' I reckon it's Bunyard,' Curley said. ' His sister's married to a German.'

' Don't be daft,' Sam said. ' He hasn't even been to France yet.'

' He has,' Curley said. ' He did two freights in *Emma*. He was rounding up to go alongside at Beckton again when the steamer hit him.'

Sam felt an unfamiliar anxiety come over him at Curley's news. The old skipper's talk in the pub about having a German for a brother was the literal truth if what Curley said was true. Sam had shaken off his misgivings at Bunyard's outspokenness during the last twelve hours, but now a horrid doubt gave his inside a twist. With the security men looking for spies, and his own skipper a self-confessed German-lover . . . Sam, hot with patriotism, stared blankly at Curley. Not for the finest freight in the fastest barge in the world would he have divulged to his friends the incident in ' The Barge '. Sam was torn with doubt. For on the passage from the Crouch, Sam had discovered that Bunyard could sail a barge better than he had known was possible; he had found Bunyard fair and even kindly, and had been looking forward to their next trip together. He did not want to believe Curley's gossip. He did not want to believe what Curley said about Bunyard's sister. Anyone with German connexions was suspect, and people with German names had been beaten up in London. Even the two Goldsmith barges, *Germanic* and *Teutonic*, had had their names changed to *Lais* and *Maymon*.

Percy and Curley started discussing why Bunyard had hit the steamer, but Sam left them angrily and went ashore to get some shopping. A big poster on a riverside wall caught his eye:

YOUR KING AND COUNTRY NEED YOU
A Call to Arms

An addition of 100,000 men to His Majesty's Regular Army is immediately necessary in the present grave National Emergency. Lord Kitchener is confident that this appeal will be at once responded to by all who have the safety of our Empire at heart.

Sam read it gravely. He remembered Manny reading it in the same place a few weeks back, and supposed Gil would read it too when he went out. He pulled his cap straight and walked on into the hot, grimy streets, where tar oozed up between the sets and little girls in grubby pinafores and button boots were playing hopscotch. The clatter and spark of heavy drays, the raucous voices of the London women and the hubbub and fug of the lunchtime alehouse came strangely after the long days and nights at sea and up the sleepy Essex rivers; he felt out of place and resentful. The conversation with Curley and Percy had disturbed him, and he knew that he had left because he didn't want to hear them suggest that Bunyard's brush with the steamer had been his own fault. Spy indeed? Sam jingled the money in his pocket. Their gossip was worse than a woman's.

He did his shopping. Nothing seemed any different, except the prices, which were all a penny or two higher. He had a meal of sausage and mash for twopence, looked at the posters outside the picture palace, bought a magazine called *The War Illustrated* and picked up a newspaper he found in the street. It had long casualty lists which he looked through, under the Gs, for Manny's name. The dead were in black and white, before his eyes, but to Sam it all seemed totally unreal. He could not picture it. He did not expect Manny to be killed, and when he thought of himself as a soldier,

he did not think of dying as a soldier. The news was always of British victories. He could not think why the casualty lists were so long, for victories.

'This time tomorrow, I could be in France,' he thought. A shiver of excitement went through him. He dropped the newspaper back in the gutter, tucked his magazine in his pocket and hurried back to the barge.

The third hand was to join the barge at Beckton when they loaded. Sam was told to keep a look-out for him, as the *Flower of Ipswich* waited her turn off the loading jetty, where the coke poured in a noisy stream out of the trucks and down the chute. Ashore the furnaces in the black retort houses roared and belched forth fire and fumes like an engraving of hell; the wagon-loads of fuel clacked and clattered on the overhead gantries. The river shimmered in the heat. Sam watched the coal-dust blowing across the deck, and felt the grit sticking to the sweat on his face. He saw a rat scutter across the mud where the shining swill of the tide ebbed and sucked under the creaking jetties. ' Stinking old London river,' he thought, and he pushed up his cap and wiped the sweat away, leaving a long black mark across his forehead.

' *Flower of Ipswich!* ' The shout floated out from the jetty.

' There he is,' said Bunyard. ' Go and get 'im. Look sharp now. They're ready for us up there.'

Sam rowed across to collect their crew who was waiting with his kit-bag. He dropped it into the rowing-boat with expert aim and swung down to join Sam.

' I timed it all wrong,' he said, grimacing at the barge which was just receiving the first of her hundred and eighty tons of coke down the chute. ' I should've come when you'd got the hatches on.'

Sam grinned. The newcomer was about seventeen, a thin, gangling boy with straight black hair, ginger-brown eyes and a very pale, angular face.

' They told me this freight's for Calais,' he said. ' That right? '

' Yes.'

' Cor blimey. Good as joining the army.'

The barge was already losing her freeboard with the weight of the coke thundering down the chute. The air was full of choking dust. Sam, who thought he had handled

some unpleasant freights in his short time—like refuse from
the Greenwich tip to Otterham Creek for brickmaking—
realized what his new shipmate meant about timing his
arrival when Bunyard handed them both a spade and told
them to get down and spread the load. The hot afternoon
degenerated into a nightmare of slithering up and down
screes of coke, sliding the flanks of the great grey
pyramid from the lip of the chute into the farthest corners of
the hold. Spitting dirt, choked and drenched in sweat, Sam
shovelled the last truckload into the last grimy corner and
stepped off the top of the pile on to the deck with a groan of
relief. Bunyard was already getting the hatch-covers on.

'One thing with Calais, boy,' he grunted to Sam, 'you
don't do your own unloading.'

The new hand, who Sam gathered was called Albert, was
coughing when he came up on deck. He seemed unable to
get his breath, and sat down on the coaming with his head
on his arms, gasping and wheezing. Sam, helping Bunyard
with the hatches, looked at him anxiously, but Bunyard
said derisively, 'Fine bit of brawn we're shipping here.' He
heaved a heavy cover into place with the ease of a man in his
prime and said, 'Are you something the army wouldn't have?'

Albert's head nodded.

'What did they say is wrong with you?'

Albert took a gasping breath. 'My eyes are the—the
wrong colour.'

Bunyard gave a guffaw and clapped Albert on the shoulder,
nearly knocking him back into the coke.

'Bit of sea air'll soon cure you, lad. Go and haul out the
topsail sheet. We've still an hour of tide we can use.'

Mooring warps were cast off and the *Flower of Ipswich*,
her deck amidships now only six inches above the water,
found the wind in her topsail and moved ponderously out
into the river. Sam hoisted the foresail, belaying the halyard
round the fore shroud, then slacked off the weather vang as

Bunyard came forward to let go the brails on the mainsail. The heavy bundles of canvas swung down into the familiar bellying spread of sail, and the *Flower of Ipswich* picked up way, making the most of a fair breeze and the last of the ebb. Albert, gradually recovering, helped Sam get all the hatch covers in place and fix the tarpaulin down with battens and wedges, then started on the inevitable deck-swabbing to clean away the coke-dust, while the skipper steered the barge through a golden grimy dusk into the damp fog of Erith Reach. Here the tide turned and the barge was anchored to await the next ebb. Bunyard retired to the skipper's cabin aft, and Sam and Albert dropped down into the crew's quarters in the fo'c'sle. After a brief meal they rolled into the dark recessed bunks and pulled up the grimy blankets. Through the forehatch the fog blew in off the Erith marshes; Sam could feel its wet throat breathing in on them, and hear the fog-horn of a stubborn coaster reverberating up through the bunkboards. Everything felt damp after the heat of the day. Sam rubbed his gritty eyes wearily, too tired to be excited about Calais. But in his familiar fo'c'sle, he became very conscious of his new companion. Albert's laboured breathing sawed the air and the occasional cough made Sam feel uneasy.

' You all right? ' he said.

' Yes,' said Albert. ' It's the fog, and that dust. Set it off, like. I'm not always bad as this.'

' Thank God for that,' Sam thought. Aloud, he said:

' You been on a barge before? '

' Yes. I been up to Yarmouth twice. My mother thought the sea would do me good. I tried to join the navy but they wouldn't have me.'

' Your mother think the navy'd do you good then? ' Sam asked, amused.

' Oh, she didn't know about that,' Albert said happily. ' She meant barges, like. So here I am.'

' I reckon your mother doesn't know barges.'

' No. But I don't tell her things. Just go in with her, keep her happy. You treat women like that.'

Sam was impressed with Albert's amiable worldliness.

' I don't mind this job,' Albert said, ' if the old chest bears up. I've worked with Bunyard before,' he added. ' Couple of years ago. I helped him unload at Rotherhithe once. He's a character.'

' Huh. He's got some funny ideas,' Sam said. ' He likes Germans.'

' His sister's married to a German.'

' Yes, I know.' Sam hesitated. ' They said on *Good Intent* that the police were round looking for spies last night.'

' Yes. I heard they were. Anything going off the coast, especially across the Channel.'

' You don't think Bunyard's a spy, do you? He's been across to France twice now. And there must be something, if the police are looking.'

' Could be anybody, couldn't it?' Albert said. ' We'll have to keep a watch-out. Make the old life more interesting, eh?'

' Yes. That's an idea. We could keep a watch-out in Calais, see if we see anything suspicious. It's terrible if there are people doing that. I don't care who it is.'

' It'd be all right to catch a spy,' Albert said, with satisfaction.

Sam lay in the darkness, thinking of the strangeness of talking about spies. A faint spasm passed through him, of a fear he could not identify. He slept, briefly, until Bunyard roused him at two in the morning.

Sam had never sailed farther south than Ramsgate. It was strange to be crashing through the choppy seas off Longnose, hardening in the sheets for the reach southward, watching for the squat grey ships that patrolled the sea passages. By dawn they had rolled past the grey towers of Reculver, by nine o'clock they were carrying the first of the flood tide in a spanking reach down to Deal. Sam began to appreciate the menace of the naval patrol when Bunyard said, ' If the beggars stop us now, I'll take up farming.' A converted trawler, white ensign flying, converged slowly on their course. Officially there for their protection, the naval patrol was considered a confounded nuisance by the barge skippers. Watching the trawler's approach, Sam was able to sympathize with Bunyard's feelings; to stop the *Flower of Ipswich* now would be enough to break a skipper's heart. She was travelling like a train, everything in her favour. With every sail set, she was scarcely heeling, but her bow-wave roared under her stem and a sheet of white foam spun from her transom like the wake of a Lipton yacht. The trawler was hard put to it to close with her, and after the captain had bawled at them through a megaphone, Bunyard freed off his sails to allow the trawler to come up.

Sam and Albert stood by warily, watching the uniformed men on the trim, converted steam-vessel, while Bunyard, still at the wheel, shouted curt answers to the captain's questions. To their great relief, after some minutes' hazardous sailing with the trawler close under their lee, the *Flower of Ipswich* was waved on, and the trawler circled away.

' And a ruddy good riddance,' Bunyard grunted.

Sam looked round thoughtfully, trying to picture the menaces that might threaten them, but it was hard to see danger in the bright, smooth sea. He remembered the vivid story of the *Amphion* which sounded like a figment of the burned sailor's imagination. Yet Sam knew it was true. He stared hard over the barge's bows to where, faint but distinct, the blue shore of France showed on the horizon, and tried to make it fit in with the closely printed lines he had been reading in his *War Illustrated*:

'Then our artillery opened fire and our soldiers in the trenches, aiming coolly and quickly, brought the Germans down in thousands. The Germans had many more guns than our force, but our deadly infantry fire helped to make a balance as the German riflemen were not good shots . . . Six attacks on the British position were made by six fresh bodies of German troops . . . whole columns of German infantry fell, and their piled up bodies blocked the streets.'

The pale shore shimmered beyond the fairest sea Sam had ever set eyes on; the sun was hot on his face. It was beyond his imagination to reconcile the fact and the writing.

Bunyard saw the magazine sticking out of his pocket, and called Sam to the wheel.

'Let's see if you can steer a course straighter than a pig's tail,' he said, and as Sam laid his hands on the wheel Bunyard took the magazine out of his pocket. He skimmed through it, and turned to the résumé of the week's events on the back page, where Sam had been reading about the German bodies. Sam, his eyes nervously flicking to the compass as he felt the heavy barge bearing up to windward, playing him up in front of Bunyard, heard Bunyard's impatient snort.

'Reads like a ruddy clay-pigeon shoot,' he said.

'It's Germans, all those bodies,' Sam said stoutly. 'That's what we want, isn't it?'

'Read on, boy,' Bunyard said. 'The result of that meeting was an allied withdrawal. An allied withdrawal sounds better than a German victory, but it means the same thing. It doesn't say so here, but if there were all those bodies belonging to the Germans, who won, how many British bodies were there after that little bloodbath? Tell me that.' He studied the magazine again, peering closely at the print, while Sam stared angrily at the compass needle, which swung away, siding with Bunyard against him. 'Here you are,' Bunyard said. '"It was during this difficult and harassing business of withdrawing with our allies that most of our losses of two thousand men appear to have occurred." That's very well put. Two thousand men appear to have been killed. Appear to have been killed.'

Sam could not tell from Bunyard's manner whether he was being sarcastic about the journalism, or whether—the seed once sown, insisted on flourishing—he was showing German sympathies. He exchanged glances with Albert, whose ginger eyes were sending out doubting looks like morse messages.

'It's a supreme honour to die for your country. It says so,' Sam said stubbornly.

'God, who taught you to steer?' Bunyard said. 'The course is southerly. We're not putting this coke off on Deal pier.'

Sam shoved the wheel over, sweating with indignation. His present task had been forgotten in his swelling gullet-choking patriotism at the thought of dying for his country. The glint of bayonets in the wash-drawings of the grubby magazine fascinated him. He glowered at Bunyard, hating him for everything.

'Two thousand bodies,' Bunyard said calmly. 'Say, four thousand, five thousand, with both sides counted. You've never seen a body, I dare say. A bloody one.'

'I saw my father after he fell down the hatch.'

'Think of five thousand. Five thousand of your supreme honours. You can't picture five thousand bodies, however hard you try. Can you?'

Sam did not answer. He was trying, but the barge was swinging off again. He wished Bunyard would leave him alone.

'You young fools. When you're as old as I am, you'll see how senseless the whole bloody thing is. I've fought in a few wars in my time. I'm so old—my father was at Waterloo. And you, you silly boy, you're the same all over again.

You'll rush off and get killed. And what good is it to be a supreme honour in print, a load of ruddy claptrap? When you can be alive and learning and growing up. For God's sake, if you don't keep this barge on course I'll put you off in Calais and leave you there.'

Bunyard stamped down the companion-way into the cabin and left Sam and Albert petrified on the deck. Sam, his eyes desperately on the compass, said, 'He's mad. He ought to be locked up.'

'He doesn't understand,' Albert said, amazed. 'He talks like a lunatic. As if us and the Germans are the same.'

'He *is* a German,' Sam said furiously. 'Good as, anyway.'

'I'll tell you what,' Albert said, 'he's a ruddy liar. If his father was at Waterloo, he must be a hundred.'

'Why, when was Waterloo?'

'Well, look. Say he's sixty-five.' Albert pulled a pencil out of his pocket and started doing sums on the margin of *The War Illustrated* which Bunyard had flung down in disgust. 'That makes him born in—er—' There was a long pause. 'Eighteen forty-nine.'

'Well, I suppose his dad could have been born in eighteen hundred. Holy Moses! His grandma could've been Nell Gwynne.'

'He's an old, mad fool,' Albert said, as if he had just proved it by his sums. 'I'm not sure when Waterloo was, but it sounds a long time back. I think he's a liar.'

'Yes, and perhaps he's the spy too,' Sam said darkly, humiliated and prepared to believe the worst. 'What've we let ourselves in for?'

He glowered at Calais, a faint blue haze off the starboard bow.

3 Sam Speaks Out

It took Sam and Albert several trips to get used to Calais.
It was frighteningly foreign, the harbour swarming with
little gesturing men shouting the incomprehensible lingo.
Trains rumbled along the dockside—strange, un-British
locomotives with unfamiliar whistles—and unloaded racks
of swathed stretchers for transference to a rust-streaked
coaster with a red and white cross painted on its side;
the tall steam-cranes clacked and clanked over the unloading bays, dashingly manoeuvred by excitable gnomes in
black berets. The harbour stank. Oil washed the greasy
steps and filmed the pale blue transom of the *Flower of
Ipswich*. The smells were different, foreign smells, and the
food was uneatable. The bread was a mile long and there
was no beer. Sam and Albert padded round the docks,
appalled.

'Cor, give me Yarmouth any day,' Albert said.

But they were away in two tides, and had no complaint to
make of the unloading and the quick turn-round. Sam and
Albert had a bottle of wine in the fo'c'sle. Sam thought of
the German mines and had a quick swig to give him courage,
but the sour, flat taste made him grimace.

'This Frog stuff—'s like bilge water.'

'They drink it all the time,' said Albert, in wonder.
'Nothing else.'

'No wonder they're all mad.'

'All foreigners are mad,' Albert said.

Three miles out from Calais, the *Flower of Ipswich* came
up with a French fishing-boat and, to the boys' surprise,
Bunyard altered course to go close to her. He called Sam to
take the wheel, and as the two craft closed he went forward

and stood by the shrouds. The French captain shouted across and Bunyard shouted back.

'What's he saying?' Sam said to Albert, watching his course. A slight turn of the wheel and a nudge with the hissing leeboard would burst the fisherman's side open at the rate they were travelling.

'He's talking Frog lingo,' Albert said, aghast.

Sam strained his ears. Whatever it was, he could not understand a word of it. The fishing-boat could not keep up with the barge, and as the *Flower of Ipswich* forged ahead the two skippers waved amicably. The fishing-boat freed off and made towards Gris Nez and Bunyard came back to the wheel, smiling to himself. Sam saw his eyes go to the compass.

'We'll make a helmsman of you yet,' the skipper said, for once finding nothing wrong, and he left Sam at the wheel while he went below and made himself something to eat. He cooked for himself in the captain's quarters aft, and Albert cooked in the fo'c'sle for himself and Sam. (Albert, Sam had discovered with pleased surprise, was a splendid cook.)

The fact that Bunyard spoke French was another mark against him in the boys' eyes.

'It's not natural,' Albert said. 'Who does he think he is?'

Sam had the suspicion that it was easy for Bunyard to have secrets if he spoke Frog. He had developed a deep distrust of Bunyard for his strange opinions, and kept thinking about the spy-hunt Curley Tompkins had talked about. He did not want to think about it, but it kept coming into his mind uninvited, every time another strangeness of Bunyard's was revealed. The old man kept himself to himself, and the age difference was so great between him and his hands that his apartness was accentuated. There was none of the grumbling and bantering that Sam had got accustomed to with his last skipper, but a far greater awareness of the skipper's authority. Sam found it a great change, and

resented being found wanting. He found he now tried very
hard to steer a good course, so that he could not be humiliated
again by Bunyard's scorn, but he resented having to try so
hard, and scowled as he stood at the wheel.

The coke trade was hard, but it paid better than any of the
other freights. By the time Christmas had come and passed,
the war, to the surprise of many prophets, was not only still
waging, but eating up an uncommon number of men,
supplies and ammunition.

'Good for trade,' Bunyard said cynically, and as the new
year got under way, the *Flower of Ipswich* was joined in her
Channel crossings by *Trilby*, *Good Intent* and several more.
Sam, an old hand, showed Gil round Calais, and Scruff had
his first fight with what Sam called a Frog-dog. Gil had had
his eighteenth birthday, and a white feather in an envelope
through the post, but made no mention of volunteering.

Once he said to Sam, 'What good would I be?' Sam
could not reply, dumb with shame for his brother. But Gil
seemed unmoved, and dropped the white feather into the
Channel, where it disappeared in the wake that *Trilby* scored
across the grey water. Sam could not understand Gil, whose
silences were inscrutable. He could not understand whether
Gil minded being a coward, or whether he wasn't aware of
being one. The one question, 'What good would I be?'
was not phrased with bitterness or self-disgust. It was
a quiet, plain question, put without expression. But Gil
must *feel*, Sam thought angrily. He could not be numb to
what people were thinking. He was supposed to be the
intelligent, sensitive Goodchild. Sam would stare at his
brother sometimes, and in Gil's dark, sea-grey eyes he would
read nothing. If Gil was frightened of enlisting, or frightened
of not enlisting, which Sam thought he must be, it did not
show.

'He's doing a good job,' Bunyard said of him once.
'What does it matter?'

But Sam already knew Bunyard was mad.

The barge life was very apart from everyday life ashore, and Sam felt strange when he went ashore in London, and even stranger when, in February, he went home for a few days to the cottage at Fambridge. Both the *Flower of Ipswich* and *Trilby* had gone into the yard at Ipswich for a refit, and the crews were given a rare holiday, three days off. Sam and Gil went home together by train, in silence. Sam felt that the green fields were now more foreign than France and wished he were away off the North Foreland, using the fair north-westerly that was blowing, but Gil was eager to see Agnes, and for once his face was animated, his eyes darting over the familiar landmarks as the train drew near home. Sam felt that this weakness for Agnes was as bad as Gil's other weakness, and sat withdrawn, scowling.

At home nothing had changed outwardly, but the village seemed empty and drab, and all women. Sam felt strange in a house, but it was pleasant enough to sit by a roaring fire with no one to shout at him, and his mother bustling round preparing a meat pie and showing him Manny's letters. They were very brief, saying he was all right and hoping she was. He was now in France, presumably fighting. Sam held the small grubby sheets of paper in his hand, looking at Manny's square, laboured writing, and felt a deep affection for Manny, and a great envy of him.

' I wish I were old enough to go,' he said to his mother.

' You daft boy. One out there is enough to worry about.'

' I suppose Gil will go first. He's old enough now.'

' There'll be plenty of time,' his mother said. ' You're doing a man's job now. What more do you want?'

' What, getting shouted at by old Bunyard?'

' They'll shout harder in the army, dearie,' his mother said drily.

Gil was out. It was a long time since Sam had been alone with his mother. He looked at her curiously. She was a tough little woman who looked older than her fifty years, with her scraped-back grey hair and thick black skirts. Since her husband had died she had kept herself by washing and cleaning in the village. The boys all sent her money when they could, which she saved against a rainy day. She had seen many rainy days in her time, and believed in being prepared. She knew that the war threatened her now, through her boys, more cruelly than anything she had yet come up against, but she had no defence against it, beyond her own stringent nature, and the knowledge that she was merely one of millions in a similar situation. She looked at Sam with pity, seeing him as pathetically young, yet nearly old enough to fight for his country.

' Where's Gil disappeared to? The pie's nearly done.'

' He went to call on Agnes Martin,' Sam said sourly.

' Oh, like that, is it? '

' He's interested in her, but I don't know if she's interested in him.'

' Agnes Martin is interested in every man in the village,' Mrs. Goodchild said tartly.

' Gil ought to have more sense,' said Sam.

' Oh, you'll be as bad, come you're eighteen.'

' Huh.' Sam was disgusted.

The next day when Sam was down on the sea-wall he saw Gil and Agnes walking along, their arms twined round each other. Not wishing to be seen, Sam stepped back behind a beached smack and watched them go by. It was a mild grey day and Agnes's shawl was thrown back; her head was lifted into the wind and she was laughing. Sam did not recognize the plump child he had known at school. This Agnes was a lovely thing, her great mass of golden-brown hair blowing in the wind. She had a radiance about her that Sam had never seen before and did not understand. Gil, throwing a stick of driftwood for the barking Scruff, was laughing too, his face animated and alight. Sam felt cut off from

them as if they were two people he did not know, so different
were they from how he thought he knew them. Gil's laugh
sent a curlew up from the saltings. Sam shrank back into the
shadow of the smack, disturbed and cross. He had never
imagined Gil being a success in his role of lover, and resented
this new picture of him, confident and laughing on the sea-
wall. When they had gone, Sam mooched along the mud,
looking at the forlorn little yachts lying in their berths,
waiting for better times. Neglected, tattered canvas covers
flapped in the breeze. Sam looked across the grey river, and
felt that it was a long time since the *Flower of Ipswich* had
been in the Crouch. Already, it seemed a long time since the
war had started.

When they went back to Ipswich, Gil was silent and sullen.
Sam was perversely pleased, and whistled as the train smoked
its way across the rolling winter fields. It was bitterly cold,
and Sam thought of the February Channel, and wondered

why he was whistling, but he kept on, to annoy Gil. Twelve hours later he was at sea again. Ahead of him, in the driving rain of the short winter day, Gil was at *Trilby's* helm, hunched indifferently against the weather. Sam knew that he would not be seeing Agnes for several weeks, and was spitefully pleased again. The two barges bit into the steep choppy seas down the Wallet, past Walton's deserted pier and the blank remote windows of Frinton. There was nothing to be seen moving anywhere, on land or sea, apart from themselves.

Albert came on board at Beckton, wheezing cheerfully, and Sam was surprised by his own pleasure at seeing him again. It seemed as if there had never been a break in the old routine, the loading, battening down, slipping away on the ebb down through the marsh mists of Plumstead and Erith, topsail sullenly pulling. At sea they saw nothing.

'Some old war,' Albert said despondently. 'Fat lot we see of it.'

Sam, who also wanted a submarine or two to talk about, but was dubious about actually being so rash as to hope for some excitement, knew what Albert meant. In Calais the rain washed about the cobbles. Albert coughed, shaking the icy drips from his coke-black cap.

'Look,' said Sam. 'There's the skipper talking to a native.'

'Old basket,' said Albert.

They hated to hear Bunyard chatting away in French. Their faces were full of suspicion. The two boys regarded the French as only slightly less sinister than the Germans, and kept themselves rigidly to themselves when in Calais. They hated Bunyard's easy fraternization.

When the *Flower of Ipswich* put out to sea again in a moderate, fair south-westerly, Bunyard told the boys to go below and get their heads down for an hour or two, until they closed with the Kentish coast. This was unusual, but the two boys were only too pleased to comply, and rolled

gratefully into their bunks. Accustomed to sleeping whenever
they got the chance, they dozed off immediately, but Sam was
awakened some time later by an instinctive awareness that
the barge had stopped sailing. He was instantly awake, and
lay tense, listening. He thought he could hear another boat
sailing close by; while the *Flower* wallowed, luffed up into
the wind, the creaking of an unfamiliar rigging came close,
filling Sam with anxiety. What on earth was Bunyard
doing?

Sam rolled out of his bunk, scrambled up the companion-
way and put his head out of the hatch. A cold drizzle swept
over him. He peered into the darkness, and made out the
rigging of the other boat alongside. She was sailing, pinched
up, but slowly overhauling the *Flower*, not a light showing
anywhere. Sam thought she was a French trawler, but
couldn't be sure. Sam heard a muffled shout from her deck,
an excited mumble of foreign voices, a quick order, and
Bunyard's voice calling something. Sam heard him clearly,
yet the words meant nothing. The *Flower* started to sail
again, and the trawler freed off and receded into the darkness. Sam stood there, his head out of the hatch, staring
bitterly into the rain, feeling it needling his sleep-warm face,
pricking all his suspicions into life.

Albert muttered something as Sam went back below,
and Sam went over and crouched down by his bunk.

' What's the old man doing? ' Albert asked, peering out
from under his blanket.

' He's been talking to some Froggie trawler again.'

' You catch anything? '

' All French. Bunyard said something that sounded like
" mare cruddy ". That's all, and the trawler cleared off.'

' What's he on about then? ' Albert propped himself up
on one elbow, his black hair dangling from its smart centre
parting, the ginger eyes peering from beneath. ' Why didn't
he want us to know? Packing us off to bed. . . . '

'Yes,' said Sam. 'That's what I was thinking. He didn't want us to know. He must've thought we'd sleep through it. And why didn't he want us to know?'

'Ve—ry suspicious,' said Albert, drawing out his syllables.

'What's it mean?' Sam asked. 'Mare cruddy. D'you know?'

'*Mère* or something is mother, isn't it?' Albert said. 'Mother Cruddy. Who's she?'

'God knows.'

'A spyess,' said Albert.

They were interrupted by a bellow from above.

'All hands!'

They pulled on their smocks, muttering, and went up into the rain. The *Flower of Ipswich* was crashing along, thudding into the steep waves whose white crests were the only gleam in the February darkness.

'You take her,' Bunyard said to Sam. 'The lantern's smoking below.'

He took Albert below with him to adjust the offending lamps, and Sam was left alone at the wheel, sour and angry. Bunyard was not very clever, he thought, getting them out of the way just until the trickery was over, and then setting them to work again as soon as it suited him, as if nothing had happened. They should have guessed something was up when he had sent them into their bunks just out of Calais. Bunyard had never been one to spare his crew. Even now, in the pitch darkness of the winter Channel, the *Flower* was carrying all her canvas. The wind was strengthening, and Sam was worried, having her all to himself in this evil darkness, the rain crackling against his jacket, the cold pinching his face. Soon, he knew, Bunyard would come up and stand behind him, his hands in his pockets. Unless it was easy conditions, Bunyard was never far from the helm. Sam shook the rain off his nose, and groaned to himself. This was one of the occasions Albert would sum up with a complacent wheeze: 'Life's not all roses, you know.'

But Albert cleaned the lamp and rehung it, and Bunyard came up and stood on deck behind Sam, and the *Flower of Ipswich* crashed on, a tide ahead of her rivals, who still lay in the basin at Calais. She was loaded again at Beckton and moored off the following evening, when *Trilby*, the *Good Intent*, *Thomas and Anne*, and *Martha* came up on the tide. Sam, watching from the foredeck, noticed that Gil was at *Trilby's* wheel, with Scotty Smith, the third hand, acting as mate. There was no sign of Harry Finch. Idly curious, Sam watched Gil put the barge about and come up to the big mooring buoys against the tide, staysail and topsail just giving him way, the mainsail brailed up, rain-black against the dusk. He went up forward to take a warp from Scotty, mentally—grudgingly—admiring Gil's judgement as *Trilby* came alongside, a mere whisper of way at her bows. Staysail and topsail were smartly handed, Sam put a turn over the *Flower's* winch and Scotty was rowing warps out to the buoys almost before *Trilby* had taken up on Sam's bowline. *Trilby*, empty, seemed to tower above the laden *Flower of Ipswich*. The other barges tied up outside *Trilby*, and Scotty and Curley Tompkins came over to ask Sam why Bunyard was in such a hurry.

'Told you he was a driver, didn't I?' Curley said cheerfully. 'You'll be drove to death come next Christmas.'

'We'll be retired by next Christmas,' Albert said. 'Rich as Rockefeller.'

'Three trips to your two,' Sam jeered. 'You want to move in that old tub.'

Curley yawned ostentatiously. 'A good night's sleep, that's what I'm looking forward to.' He grinned maliciously at Sam and Albert, who had spent the last few hours trimming coke in the hold and were expecting to sail within the next hour. Curley knew, as well as anyone, how it felt to be as tired as Sam and Albert. 'You can keep your drivers. Give me a skipper that's human.'

' What's happened to your skipper?' Sam asked Scotty, ignoring Curley's jibe. ' Since when has Gil been promoted?'

' Most of the trip. Finch scalded his foot on the way out. Boiling kettle went over it, and he's laid up. Can't get out of his bunk. He says it's mending, pig-headed old devil. Won't go ashore to get it seen to, so we've got to do all the work. And that brother of yours is as bad-tempered as they come.' Scotty stared accusingly at Sam, as if it were his fault. ' What's got into him lately? Proper moody he's turned.'

' Gil?' Sam was surprised. Then he remembered. He gave a derisive guffaw. ' Of course! He's in love! That's his trouble. He'll be pining for his Agnes, and taking it out on you. Poor old Gil!'

' No! Is *that* his trouble? Cor, strike me!'

The boys all doubled up with roars of laughter, until a fierce shout told them Bunyard had come back with his clearance papers and was ready to go. They scattered, Sam and Albert to work and Curley and Scotty, stretching and yawning with gleeful exaggeration, to their bunks.

The next time the *Flower of Ipswich* left Calais, Sam and Albert were once again offered the watch below, and the *Flower* went alongside the French trawler a few miles offshore. This time Sam and Albert were not asleep, but waiting for this rendezvous to occur. Albert had even worked out the significance of Mother Cruddy, the arch-spy.

' Mère Cruddy!—*Mercredi*. It's French for Wednesday! That's what you heard!'

'Today's Wednesday,' said Sam.

' Well, that's it then. That's what he was telling 'em. Meet you on Wednesday.'

' What for?' said Sam darkly.

' We'll ask him,' Albert said.

But when the *Flower of Ipswich* had duly exchanged words

with the trawler and gone on her way, Sam and Albert, deeply disturbed, shied from accusing Bunyard of treachery.

'What do we say?' Sam moaned softly. 'I don't know about you, but I'd rather jump overboard than ask him.'

'Coward,' Albert said.

'You ask him.'

Albert did not reply.

'But what's he up to?' Sam said, after a long pause. 'How do we find out?'

'Come to think of it, asking him's not the best way. He could tell us anything. We ought to watch, next time it happens. See what we can see. Catch him red-handed.'

Sam thought this over. Albert was making an excuse for not asking Bunyard now, himself, but his idea was acceptable to Sam. It didn't mean they weren't going to do anything about it, but they didn't have to do anything immediately.

The momentous decision taken, the boys had no opportunity to put the plan into practice, for on the next trip, and the next, Bunyard stopped for no one. The crew were offered no watches below, not much relief of any kind. The weather was bitter. Sam watched the grey seas for the porpoise heave of a mine, very much aware of the war, very solemn, as he thought of Manny somewhere—not so many miles away—amongst the inferno that even he had been able to hear from the French coast. Faint, distant reverberations had shivered the *Flower's* rigging as she had lain in the basin in Calais. Sam's copy of *The War Illustrated* called it 'Neuve Chapelle's Immortal Story', but Sam for all his fervour, did not want Manny immortalized. There was a little piece in the close print that even he had read twice; in fact more than twice. He could remember it, word for word, as he stood on the deck. It was about 'the Immortal Division, the Seventh' and it said, 'Since losing nearly five men out of every six, in the greatest achievement in our history, it had reorganized, and its scanty veterans

filled the new drafts with their high spirit. . . .' Sam knew
that Manny was in the Seventh, but he didn't know whether,
after six months, he counted as a veteran. But if a man had
seen five out of every six of his companions die, how could
he not be a veteran? A little vein of Bunyard's thinking,
unbidden, ran through Sam's mind: how could losing five
men out of every six be the greatest achievement in history?
Sam blew on his frozen fingers, anxious for Manny, anxious
for his own convictions that, ever so slightly, he realized,
had been undermined by Bunyard's scorn. Since hearing the
guns, the war had come very close. Calais, in the never-
ending rain, was full of hospital trains and the ships with the
red crosses, and schools and churches and crypts had been
turned into shelters and hospitals. Sam shook the rain off his
sou'wester and stamped his cold feet.

When they anchored off Gravesend to await the next
flood, a letter was passed to Sam from a barge just down
from Battlesbridge. It was from his mother and said, ' Manny
is safe, thank God. I have a letter from him. He is sick with
a fever and is safe in a camp. I never thought till now that a
fever could be a blessing. Look after yourselves, dear boys.
Gil, you forget that Agnes Martin. She is no good and I
have told her so. God bless you.'

Sam read it with a feeling of relief, slightly tinged with
disappointment. He had not wanted Manny killed, but being
sick with a fever sounded dull, in the midst of an ' immortal
story '.

The mate, Josh, who had given Sam the letter, came
from Burnham, not far from Sam's home village. Sam
went ashore for a drink with him at the ' Ship and
Lobster '.

' Your old ma, she comes up to Battlesbridge in the
carrier's cart, to give it me. She knew we were bound for
London. She wanted you to know your brother was all
right, she said.'

Sam chuckled. 'The last bit'll please Gil, won't it? I bet it'll worry him more than he worried about Manny.'

Sam showed the letter to Josh.

'Oh, aye, Agnes Martin, I know her,' Josh said. 'There's few men our way who don't,' he added. 'Your ma's quite right.'

Sam shrugged. By the time he had finished his pint, Gil had come in with a limping Harry Finch, and their third hand Scotty. Gil would not have acknowledged Sam, but Sam took the letter across to him.

'What is it?'

'It's from Ma. Josh brought it down.'

Gil backed out of the crush at the bar and stood in a corner, shaking the letter straight with one hand, his beer in the other. Sam watched him as he read it. Right behind Gil's head was a poster of Kitchener pointing his imperious finger, with the caption, 'Your Country Needs You'.

The accusing finger stabbed between Gil's shoulder-blades and Kitchener's cold eyes bored into the back of Gil's neck. Sam, fascinated by the appropriateness of the publican's bill posting, almost expected Gil to be aware of the Field-Marshal's injunction, and to give some sign, but Gil's thoughts were obviously not, at that moment, with his country. Sam was startled to see his mild face suffuse with colour. His hand clenched on the letter.

'The interfering old woman!' he hissed bitterly. 'Who told *her* about Agnes?'

He glared at Sam, who was frightened by his venom. There was a desperate anger in Gil's eyes that Sam had never guessed his brother capable of.

'It was no secret, was it?' Sam said balefully.

'I'll strangle her if she's spoken to Agnes!' Gil said. He crushed the letter in his hand and drank down his beer in furious gulps. Sam noticed that the angry colour was right down his neck and in his ears, so that the thick golden-red hair seemed to flame with the suffusion beneath it. But his eyes were as cold as the North Sea.

He flung his glass down on a table, and with a curt command to Scruff, pushed his way through the crush and out of the door. The little dog hopped to clear his tail as the door slammed, and they were gone. Sam was astonished.

' Where's he gone? ' Josh asked.

' Don't ask me! ' Sam said. He felt worried. ' This Agnes Martin he's so daft about, what's wrong with her, then?'

Josh leered at him. ' You're too little,' he said. ' Kids like you don't know about women.' Then, as Sam looked at him impatiently, he stopped his banter and said, ' There's no harm in her, save she likes a lot of men. Especially if they've got plenty of money. Last I heard she was going with George Young. He's in munitions, and you know what sort of a pay-packet they take home.'

' Gil's not rich. Why'd she go with him then?'

' Finding out, I dare say. If he wants her, he'll have to make money, that's for sure. More than barging'll give him.'

' The coke pays well.'

' Better than flour and stuff, perhaps. But not better than making munitions. That's the line. Good, safe job and plenty of cash. It's only fools as volunteer.'

Sam glared at Josh. 'I'm volunteering soon as I'm old enough! Manny's gone. It makes me mad that Gil doesn't go. It's no excuse, being mate on a barge.'

Josh was grinning. 'As a matter of fact, I'm going when this trip's finished. If the navy will have me. I fancy a trip foreign, the old Dardanelles'ld suit me nice.'

Sam was filled with envy. 'D'you think, if I said I was eighteen—?'

'You? You don't look eighteen, not by a long chalk.' Josh laughed.

Sam was left disappointed, and vaguely worried about Gil's reaction to the letter. He couldn't understand Gil. At one o'clock in the morning, when the tide was flooding again and the barges started to make sail for the last leg up to Beckton, Sam was surprised when Harry Finch bawled across the water: 'Sam Goodchild! Where's your ruddy brother gone?'

Albert said, 'What's he talking about?'

'God knows,' said Sam, and bawled back a negative answer.

Bunyard shouted at him to set the topsail, and in the darkness, numbed with cold, Sam fumbled for the halyards. Something was jammed aloft; Bunyard swore, and Sam had to go up the ratlines, shrinking as the cold wind bit his face, cursing and muttering, wondering if Gil had gone home to strangle their mother. Gravesend lay black alongside, slumbering up its hill, tomblike as its name, but away beyond, like needles darning a pattern, the searchlights weaved the sky. Sam, aloft, felt an affinity with them, divorced from the toil and dirt of the river and town. They were beautiful, in their eerie, ominous way. A train hooted from the Tilbury side, like a town owl on the hunt. Sam could see the glow from its boiler but the sheds and the warehouses and the docks were all in darkness, hiding.

'For God's sake! Are you asleep up there!'

Bunyard's voice brought him, literally, back to earth.

Gil did not turn up till the following evening, when *Trilby* was just about to sail. He said nothing about where he had been, but stood expressionless as Finch shouted at him. Sam looked on curiously—the *Flower of Ipswich* lay alongside —but Gil showed no remorse, nor guilt. His face was like a stone. When Finch had finished, Gil shrugged. Sam saw the contempt. He could not understand Gil, nor did he understand why Finch, recognizing the contempt, said no more.

Two weeks later Calais was bombed by the German airships, and Sam and Albert had their first experience of war close at hand. They did not like it. Sam had not known that he could be so frightened. He stood on the *Flower's* deck with Albert, mesmerized by the sight of the shining, unnatural object hanging over the rooftops. The next moment a sinister, crescendoing whine filled the sky, and Sam, with an alacrity he did not know he possessed, jumped down the companion-way into the forepeak and threw himself into the dark recesses of his bunk. The noise he had read about so often in *The War Illustrated* had caught up with him: ' the high screaming note ' and the ' crash like thunder ' shook the old barge as if she had gone aground, and Sam put his head under the pillow. Later, chastened, he watched the French excitement, the fantastic Gallic gabbling, the running and shouting, the passage of the motor-bike ambulance with its two side-car stretchers carrying bloody bundles wrapped in blankets. The smell of dust and cordite drifted over the harbour. The railway station, they said, was in ruins. Sam felt cold and shocked. He was glad when the *Flower* was unloaded and they were able to lock out and put the widening water between themselves and the excited port. It was going dusk. Almost immediately, Bunyard told Sam and Albert they could have a spell below.

Sam's satisfaction disappeared with the order. All the old

doubts came tumbling back into his mind. He went down into the forepeak and looked at Albert grimly.

'What was your plan then? We watch him?'

'Something like that,' Albert said tentatively. 'See if they pass anything, or just talk.'

'We can't understand the talk anyway. There must be more to it than just talk.'

'Yes. Well, we'll see.'

They lay on their bunks, staring up at the deck beams, listening to the heavy pounding of the Channel waves. Sam lost count of time. The *Flower*, unladen, was slamming the sea with uneasy plunges; mast, sprit and shrouds groaned and shivered above them. Knockings and drippings, thuds and shudders punctuated the incessant motion. The barge was beating, close-hauled, into a wind that would rather take them back to Calais than out to the white cliffs of Kent, and she was complaining with all cantankerousness that Sam expected of the female sex. Sam braced himself in the bunk, trying to hear above the barge's motion the approach of the expected trawler. Six times Albert said he heard it, before a distant shout proved him right.

'Come on!'

Sam padded up the companion-way steps and stuck his head out.

'Go on,' said Albert, beneath him on the steps. 'We won't see much from here.'

Bunyard was at the wheel, about fifty feet away.

'There's no law against us going on deck,' Albert was arguing, as if to convince himself.

'All right,' said Sam crossly.

He was frightened, and the fact annoyed him. Like when he saw the Zeppelin. He wanted to be intrepid, full of courage, like a soldier, not creeping with goose-pimples. He was as bad as Gil. Closely followed by Albert, he crawled up the deck, keeping his head below the level of the hatch coamings. The water soaked through the knees of his trousers and soggily permeated his warm thick socks, and he was quite conscious of the fact, which annoyed him still more. Prepared to catch a spy, red-handed, surely he should be oblivious of physical discomfort?

' That's far enough,' he thought. If he craned his neck he would see Bunyard at the wheel, and he was comforted by the thought that, in this sea, Bunyard was unlikely to leave the helm, whatever the trawler wanted to pass to him, or receive, or say. The trawler was closing on the *Flower's* lee —Sam peered out round the side of the hold and saw the dark tower of her staysail looming, and Bunyard watching her. A man was standing on the trawler's bows. There was a shout, and the man threw something which landed near Bunyard with a crunching thud, and rolled to within an arm's length of Sam. It was a large, roundish object, from which Sam hastily retreated, his damp feet colliding with Albert's face.

' All right! All right! ' Albert was muttering.

Bunyard was shouting something incomprehensible and waving cheerfully after the now departing trawler; his mysterious parcel, having rolled down to the bulwarks, lay gently rocking. Sam and Albert retreated back to the mast, and sat with their backs to the hold to consider the situation.

' Go and ask him what it is,' Albert said to Sam.

' You,' said Sam, miserably.

' I thought you were going to catch him red-handed,' Albert said indignantly. ' 's too late now. For red-handed, at any rate.'

' It nearly knocked me out, whatever it is,' Sam said.

' You should have fielded it. Chance of a lifetime,' said Albert. ' Go on, go and ask him.'

' I'll go and put my boots on,' Sam said.

He went below and put his boots and smock on, feeling trapped. He could not understand why he felt so frightened.

He went back on deck and walked aft as if his boots were filled with lead. The parcel was still lying where he had last seen it. He walked up to the wheel, and Bunyard said, ' Good. You can have her for a bit. The course is north-east.'

' North-east,' said Sam.

He took the wheel and looked at the compass. Bunyard picked up the round parcel and went below with it. Albert came down the deck and looked closely at Sam.

' What did he say?' he whispered heavily.

' He said, " You can have her for a bit. The course is north-east," ' Sam said.

' God Almighty!' said Albert. ' Is that all?'

Sam nodded.

' And what did you say?'

Sam was silent.

' Nothing?'

Sam nodded.

At dawn, the *Flower of Ipswich* anchored in the Downs to await her tide. Albert had put the kettle on in the captain's quarters and Bunyard told them to get below and get a drink before they went to their bunks. Shedding smocks, they crowded into the snug cabin where the coal-stove glowed and the kettle steamed.

' Good as the Ritz,' Albert said appreciatively.

Bunyard followed them, and got out the cups and teapot.

' Make a thick brew, lad,' he said to Albert. ' None of your dish-water.'

Sam sat screwing up his poor courage, aware that if he did not say anything now, the Goodchild courage would be vested in Manny alone, and he would be able to consider himself no better than Gil. The burden of this realization would be intolerable.

' Mr. Bunyard,' Sam said. ' Why do you keep meeting up with that French trawler?'

He stared down at his boots as he spoke, but his voice seemed to ring through the small cabin. Albert, in the middle of pouring the tea, sent a jet of smoking amber over his own wrist and gasped with pain. Bunyard looked at Sam carefully.

' He's a friend of mine.'

' But what was in the parcel he—he chucked over?' Sam, his ears burning, lifted his head and saw Bunyard considering him across the cabin table. The red veins stood out in Bunyard's cheeks, and drops of rain still stood on his big white moustache. But he did not look guilty, only amused.

' You're a nosy lad, aren't you?' he commented.

Sam nodded doggedly. ' We want to know,' he said.

Bunyard turned round and ferreted in the bunk behind him. He pulled out a bottle of cognac, which he set on the table.

' Top the tea up with that, Albert.'

Sam stared at the bottle. ' You mean—?'

Bunyard was laughing. ' Four bottles, packed with plenty of straw. Disappointed?'

Albert gave a disgusted wheeze, and started to prise off the seal.

' We thought you was a spy, at least,' Sam said.

Bunyard's expression changed. The amusement went out of his eyes and he looked at the boys closely. ' You thought I was a spy?'

' Yes,' said Albert.

Bunyard took the opened bottle and filled his mug to the rim with brandy. ' You've a lot to learn,' he said, ' about human nature.'

' They say it's going on,' Sam said. ' We were keeping our eyes open, to see if we could find out anything.'

Bunyard was silent. Sam looked at the brandy bottle, feeling let down, and very tired. After all, had he wanted

Bunyard to be a spy? He glanced at the old man again, and saw that he, too, looked very tired, and old, and withdrawn.

'That Frenchman is crazy,' Bunyard said. 'Harmless enough. He thinks he owes me something—I got him out of trouble once, a long time ago, and he likes to give me bottles of cognac. My old crew thought I was an old fool, humouring him. They said he'd knock the side out of the barge one of these days, so I thought I wouldn't give you two the chance to call me an old fool. Send you below, I thought. Why should I mind if he likes to give me some bottles of cognac? I like cognac, and it makes him happy.' Bunyard smiled, a little sheepishly. 'But this other thing—spying—' His expression changed. 'You want to be careful.'

'It *is* happening—'

'There are a few around the harbour, in Calais, who will do anything for money. And perhaps there are ships going into Calais who will carry messages—no more than that. I don't know.'

'Do you know anyone in Calais like that? You know them there. What do they say?'

'The skipper of the trawler *Notre Dame de Calais* is—' Bunyard hesitated. A heavy sigh, half yawn, interrupted his sentence, and he seemed to lose the gist of what he was saying. Or had he changed his mind?

'Is what?'

'Is—is a very lucky man, to have a brand-new steam trawler like the *Notre Dame de Calais*,' Bunyard said. Sam saw his eyes, mocking.

'That isn't what you were going to say.'

'No.' Bunyard was deadly serious. 'You don't want to know anything, or go stirring up trouble. There is enough trouble. You are hot-headed lads. You'll learn sense in time, if you're spared. Now clear up these mugs and get off to bed while you've got the chance.'

Sam and Albert did as they were told. Utterly weary,

mazed with cognac, Sam only remembered one thing
clearly of the conversation in the skipper's quarters.

'Do you know what?' he said, heaving the blanket over
his shoulder and burying his face gratefully into his pillow.
'When I said we thought he was a spy—'

'What?'

'He was hurt,' Sam said. 'Poor old beggar.'

4 'Chez Jules'

Sam gave Albert a violent nudge.

'Look!'

They were standing on the *Flower*'s bows as she was being warped through the lock-gates at Calais into an inner basin. The usual excitable gang of jabbering Frenchmen ran along the top of the lock, shouting orders that nobody understood, flinging warps and fenders with the abandon that had prompted Albert to call locking-in 'The Pantomime. Act One.' (Act Two was the unloading and Act Three the locking-out.) Sam and Albert still regarded all Frenchmen as mad.

'What's up?' said Albert.

'That trawler,' said Sam.

A big fishing-trawler was ahead of them, unusually clean and well-found, with gleaming decks, and a vast spread of red canvas neatly stowed. On her foredeck a business-like two pounder was mounted. Her name was painted with much elaborate decoration across her transom: *La Notre Dame de Calais.*

'You remember—?'

'Aye,' Albert whispered, his eyes going round and awed. 'The one Bunyard changed his mind about.'

'But I'm sure he was going to say—'

'Yes, so'm I,' Albert said.

'Attention, "Flower of EEpswich!"' A warp fell on top of them and they leapt into action, checking the barge's way while Bunyard roared from the wheel and the little Frenchmen screamed in support. Calais, now designated victualling centre for the British army in France, was one vast confusion of ships coming and going, fishing-smacks and shabby merchantmen, barges and hospital ships, damaged mine-sweepers and ammunition barges. The steam cranes were working overtime, the noisy traction lorries queuing up to receive their loads, jerked over the cobbled quays. And all the time the trains unloaded the wounded from the front: ' Calais's biggest export ' as Bunyard called it. ' Even more than fish.' It was April and ' better killing weather ', Bunyard said.

When the *Flower of Ipswich* was berthed, and Sam and Albert had been roundly cursed for their inadequacy and sharply dismissed to bed, they noticed that the *Notre Dame de Calais* was lying two boats ahead against the harbour wall, and curiosity got the better of them.

' Let's go and have a look at her,' Sam said. ' The old man's gone ashore. He won't see us.'

' It can't do any harm, to have a look,' Albert said.

They stepped on to the quayside and shuffled rather furtively, hands in pockets, to where the warps of the *Notre Dame de Calais* lay over the bollards. Several men were clearing up on board. After a few minutes' observation, Sam and Albert were able to pick out the skipper, a wiry, sharp-featured individual smoking a cheroot, addressed by the others as Jules.

' Jool? ' Sam frowned.

' Jules,' Albert said. ' It's French. What d'you think? You don't expect them to be called Archibald or Charlie, do you? '

' Jools. It's a daft name,' said Sam.

' Daft as Sam. Look, he's coming ashore.'

The skipper, biting on the cheroot, stepped up on to the quay and set off across the cobbles. As one, Sam and Albert wheeled and followed him.

' What are we doing? ' Sam muttered.

' I'm doing just what you're doing,' Albert said. ' You tell me.'

' Well, there's no harm in it, just walking along,' Sam said.

'Just walking about,' Albert agreed. 'For the fresh air.'

'We didn't get enough coming over.'

'No.'

Jules had a quick, ducking walk, head down and no loitering. He acknowledged several people with a nod or a word, but did not stop, threading his way through the traffic and confusion of the quaysides, and down the narrow street into the big cobbled square of the Place d'Armes.

'Now what?' said Sam.

The skipper crossed the square and went into a small café, one of several which all looked alike to the two boys: dark and poky under a tattered striped awning, a few iron tables and uncomfortable chairs outside, and inside a polished bar with a potted plant, more iron chairs and tables and much decorated mirror-glass, with a tariff stuck on it and a young barmaid smoothing her eyebrows into shape. The café was called 'Chez Jules'.

'It's his place then,' Albert said.

They walked past the doorway, and saw that Jules had gone behind the bar and was already in a new role of patron, talking to two men who were drinking at a table. He had made no sign to indicate that he knew of Sam's and Albert's existence, but the boys had no desire to push their luck any further. They set off back to the barge, neither of them quite sure what he had achieved.

'We know where he lives then,' Sam said.

'Yes, but we don't know anything else, do we? Not even what we followed him for?'

'Ah, well,' said Sam.

He was beginning to think that he wasn't cut out for a spy-hunter. He yawned. What had he wanted? He did not know. He went back to the *Flower* with Albert and slept.

April brought fine weather, but little else to cheer. Sam and Albert heard that the barges were to be switched from

coke to ammunition. ' And even a bargeload of shells won't last five minutes the rate they're going,' Bunyard said, and in the quiet of a spring evening, slipping towards the Calais piers with a sea the colour of amethyst, the crew on board the *Flower* could feel the shiver of distant explosions. The Germans were trying to advance, to gain control of Calais. A place called Ypres (familiarly pronounced Wipers) was constantly in the news, along with pages and pages of closely-printed Rolls of Honour. The names of the dead were so many that Sam could not make sense of them; the small print blurred; the imagination would not work. There was talk of the Germans using a deadly, poisonous gas that killed as it was carried on the April breeze. Sam strained his ears for the distant shiver of guns, but all he heard was the rustle of water under the *Flower's* bows. To be in the sun, sailing on this glittering moat that isolated England from the carnage beyond Calais, was as strange, as unbelievable as it would have been to read Manny's name amongst the printed dead: Sam could not understand, sometimes, how life could go on the same for him, day after day, working the barge, when only a few miles away all the terrible, glorious stories of the war were taking place in fact. In London he went to the recruiting centre and gave his age as eighteen. The place was not very full, and the recruiting sergeant had time to stare him up and down. Sam was wiry and strong, but not big for his years, and his face had a boy's eagerness that was his undoing.

' You're only a lad. Come back next year. Or bring me proof of your age.'

Sam was disgusted. He went home for the week-end, as Bunyard had decided to take a couple of days off. He did not tell his mother where he had been.

' You might as well be with Manny, for all I see of you,' his mother told him. ' This is only the second time since last summer. How is it Gil gets so much more time off than you? '

' Gil? How do you mean? '

' He's been down twice in the last month.'

' Gil has? ' Sam was surprised. ' How does he manage that then? '

' He didn't say.'

Sam knew Gil had been home the night he disappeared so promptly from the pub in Gravesend, and he had noticed that Gil had not been on board the last time *Trilby* had loaded at Beckton.

' He comes to see Agnes then? I didn't know how he gets away with it—with his skipper, I mean.'

' I knew it wasn't me he came to see,' Mrs. Goodchild said tartly.

Sam remembered Gil's contempt, the time Finch had rated him for leaving the barge. He wondered why Finch hadn't given Gil the sack, if he was in the habit of jumping ship. Perhaps if Gil got the sack he would enlist. Sam sighed.

' Gil . . .' he growled.

' He's a good boy. Too good for that Agnes,' said his mother. ' He brings her presents, more'n he ever brought me. Last time he brought her a fur tie, and when he'd gone back I saw her out wearing it—with George Young. But you can't tell Gil anything against her.'

' Why doesn't George join up? '

' He's working in munitions.'

' Huh. So'm I, next month. We're carrying ammunition instead of coke.'

' Oh, Sam! Is that so? ' His mother looked at him in alarm. ' And Gil too? '

' I suppose so, if he doesn't get the sack first.'

' Oh, dear.'

' What's " oh, dear " about it? '

' It's dangerous. Living on top of a load of ammunition.'

Sam sighed again, irritably.

A few days later a Zeppelin came over and dropped bombs on Ipswich. A week after that, on 7 May, 1915, a German U-boat sank the *Lusitania*, a passenger ship crossing the Atlantic from New York, and over a thousand people, including many women and children, were drowned. This incident roused an indignation that the routine killing in France had failed to do, and the recruiting offices were filled again to the doors. Sam watched Gil for signs of weakening, but Gil made no move. Sam asked Scotty if Gil ever said anything about enlisting, but Scotty shook his head.

'He wouldn't lose anything,' Scotty said. 'There's as much fighting goes on on board this barge as over in France. Old Finch and Gil are always on at each other.'

'Whatever do you mean?'

'They're always arguing,' Scotty said. 'They're both as bad-tempered as a pair of old women.'

'But surely Gil can't argue with his skipper?' Sam said, imagining himself doing the same. 'What do they argue about?'

'I dunno. They don't do it in front of me. Only down in the skipper's quarters. I hear 'em swearing at each other.'

Sam was sceptical. 'Why, Finch'd give Gil the sack, surely, if he talked back?'

'Who else'd he get, as good as Gil, if he did? I reckon Gil can handle the barge as well as Finch, better, in fact. And he does too—Finch is a lazy swine. Gil does most of the work on board, Gil and me. I don't know why he sticks it.'

Sam shook his head. 'I can't make Gil out. It must be this woman, turning him daft.'

'Yes. He goes off to see her when he's supposed to be loading. *And* he gets away with it! He's crazy about her.'

'Crazy! He's crazy all right,' Sam said scornfully.

Sam watched Gil the next time they were in the 'Ship and Lobster' off Gravesend. Everyone was grumbling about Lloyd George's new taxes on beer, but nobody was drinking any the less for it. Gil seemed to be in a good enough humour, but Sam, studying him, saw a restlessness, a touchiness, that was new. Gil had always been moody, but sullen in his off-moods, rather than aggressive. Now he seemed on edge, and ready to bite anyone's head off if he was offended. Sam thought, 'It's his conscience troubling him. If he volunteered, he'd be all right.' But when they left the pub and passed the recruiting offices with their posters, Gil looked at them blankly, unmoved. Sam stared at Gil with Kitchener's eyes, willing him to hesitate, to talk to the recruiting sergeant, but Gil merely grinned and said, ' I'm on my way to France right now, mate,' and rowed out to *Trilby*.

Bunyard was in a bad temper, having had his house in Wapping stoned and defaced by one of the mobs who were currently attacking anyone suspected of German connexions. Bunyard's German brother-in-law, a seventy-year-old chicken farmer in the Black Forest, was the cause of Bunyard's unpopularity. Sam recognized his own prejudice against Bunyard in the hysteria of the louts who wrecked his house, and was chastened.

' They shouldn't have done that,' he said to Albert.

Albert dropped his eyes guiltily. ' No. He's not a bad old beggar. Not like they think.'

They sailed for Calais, where several barges were waiting to unload ahead of them, and chaos prevailed along the overworked quays.

' Bunyard says we go to Boulogne when we go over to ammunition,' Albert said. ' It'll be better than this dump, perhaps.'

' Perhaps,' Sam growled.

The prospect of delay depressed them. They slept, but the *Flower of Ipswich* was still fourth in the queue. *Good Intent* and *Trilby* locked in on the next tide, but their crews turned in to rest, and Sam and Albert mooched about the quays aimlessly, muttering about the absence of good British beer.

' How about a pint of *du vin*? ' Albert asked.

' Dyoo van yourself,' Sam muttered. ' Cold tea'd be better.'

An idea struck him. ' How about a visit to Jules's café? See what we can see.'

' What, for a drink?'

' No, just walk past like.'

' Heavy disguise called for. Just wait while I fetch my black beard and false eyebrows.'

'Oh, shut up,' Sam growled. 'It's only for a walk somewhere.'

'Forward,' said Albert agreeably.

They strolled across the warm quays, past the clanking steam lorries with their sweating drivers bouncing to the jolt of solid tyres on worn cobbles, and the humbler but no less busy wagons pulled by dull-eyed Flanders nags, whose less fortunate brothers were being slain on the front. The smell of fire and horse-sweat and oil swilled the harbour. It was completely familiar now to the two boys, along with the smell of garlic and French bread and Gaulois cigarettes. They stuffed their hands in their pockets and pulled their caps well down against their ears, aware of being marked British as they walked along, and not wanting it any different. Their faces showed no expression. They went out into the Place d'Armes and crossed to the corner where 'Chez Jules' disported its faded awning under a thin plane-tree. The chain curtain that hung down in front of the door to keep the flies out—Jules obviously considered it summer— swung gently as the two boys went past. It was difficult to see in. Sam stopped and pretended to do up his bootlace, and peered from under the peak of his cap. He saw the tiled floor with sawdust on it, and a small dog lying under the bar. The dog looked at him and wagged his tail. Sam stared.

'Come on, you nut,' Albert said awkwardly, caught without anything to do. 'You look like ruddy Sherlock Holmes himself.'

He walked on, and Sam followed.

'What did you see?' Albert said.

'A dog,' Sam said.

Albert looked at him. 'What's up with you? What's the matter?'

'It was Scruff,' Sam said. His voice was hoarse, almost strangled. 'Scruff was lying on the floor.'

Albert stopped and his red-brown eyes stared blankly at

Sam. Sam stood, forgetting all pretence, in the middle of the pavement, his face as white as a sheet.

' Gil's dog, you mean? ' Albert said.

' Yes.'

Albert took Sam by the arm. ' We can't stand here. Come on, you daft thing.'

' But what's Gil's dog doing there? ' Sam said, propelled along by Albert. ' It means Gil's there, and what's Gil doing there? '

' You didn't see him? '

' No, but that dog goes everywhere with Gil. Gil must be there.'

' Oh, I don't know,' Albert said. ' There might be a bitch there the dog has an eye for.'

' Gil must be there,' Sam repeated.

' But *Trilby's* only just locked in. We saw him. They all went below.'

' He could have gone ashore without our seeing. We didn't watch afterwards.'

' I bet you Gil's fast asleep in the fo'c'sle. We can go and have a look and find out. Anyway, there's stacks of dogs the image of that mongrel of his. I reckon you were seeing things.'

' It was Scruff.'

' Well, what if it was, anyway? Gil's gone for a drink.'

' Why there? ' Sam asked. His voice cracked in a way he thought he had finished with. Their conversation had been very rapid, and they had been walking quickly, darting between pedestrians and vehicles. Albert was breathless and wheezing slightly and locks of his black hair were falling anxiously over his eyes.

' Why not there? ' he said flatly. ' We don't know there's anything wrong with the place. It's only guessing. Bunyard never said anything about Jules. It was only us guessing.'

Sam growled under his breath, hurrying back to the

barges. His face was stiff with shock, his eyes flaring. He ran past the cranes, ducking his way through the wagons, cursed by the dockers, and Albert wheezed in pursuit. *Trilby* lay apparently deserted, against the wall. Sam jumped down on to her deck and went to the forehatch. Albert watched him from the quay.

' Scotty! '

Sam disappeared below. A minute later he reappeared, hurried along the deck to the after-hatch and dropped down into the skipper's quarters. Albert waited.

' Well? '

Sam clambered back on to the quay and shook his head.

' He's not there? ' Albert inquired.

' No.'

' What about Scotty and Finch? '

' Yes. They've turned in. Finch said Gil's gone to see a girl. But that's a lie.'

' Jules might have a daughter. Why not? '

' But why Jules's place? ' Sam said. He turned to Albert with sudden venom, white-faced, eyes spitting, like the ' proper little fox ' Bunyard had once called him. ' Why there? ' he said, his voice breaking again. ' Why there, in the whole of Calais? *Why there?* '

5 Sam Meddles

'I shall follow him,' Sam said. 'This time I shall follow him.'

'We're sailing in the small hours, remember,' Albert said. 'You'd do better to get some sleep in. All this won't do you any good, one way or the other.'

The two boys stood on one of the Calais piers, watching *Trilby* reaching in under topsail and mizzen. It was just going dusk. The deeply-laden barge under a wind-streaked grey sky heeled between the piers, the water streaming over her decks. A heavy sea was running outside, white-flecked to a spring gale, the hard sky telling more wind. Gil was at the wheel, and Scotty stood by the mast waiting to let go the outhaul when he got the word. Of Finch there was no

sign. This was the first time Sam had set eyes on his brother
since his first visit to ' Chez Jules ' five days ago, and as the
big barge slipped past he watched Gil closely, scowling at
his competence. Finch was said to be drunk most of the time,
and Gil skipper in all but name, but no one understood why
he made no move to legalize the change-over with the
barge's Guv'nor at home, and claim the skipper's two-thirds
pay. The relationship between the two men was a strange
one, if Scotty's tales were anything to go by. Sam thought,
if his suspicions were true, he knew the reason why, but the
possibility was a black pit in his mind which he was too
frightened to explore. The thought of it brought him out
in a cold sweat. Even now, with Albert being sensible and
stolid beside him, Sam felt himself isolated in this private
hell. Albert had declined to share his suspicions. Sam watched
Gil coldly, close enough to have called to him, close enough
for Gil not to have been aware of him. But Gil made no
sign. He steered *Trilby* into the harbour and made fast
outside the lock gates. Sam and Albert followed him round,
and went beyond to where the *Flower of Ipswich* lay inside
the lock, unloaded and ready to sail. Behind her the crew of
the trawler *La Notre Dame de Calais* were making ready to
go out on the same tide at two in the morning, but there was
no sign of her skipper. From where they stood, the two boys
could watch *Trilby* without being seen.

' If he leaves the barge I'm going to follow him,' Sam
said.

' You're daft,' Albert said.

Gil and Scotty were putting out their warps. Gil moved
wearily, saying little. When the work was done, Scotty
dropped down into the forepeak, but Gil walked back aft
and disappeared into the skipper's quarters. Sam and Albert
waited.

' He's gone to kip,' Albert said. ' I knew he would.'

' I'll wait,' Sam said briefly.

Albert shrugged, and went back aboard the *Flower of Ipswich*, but Sam stood stubbornly in the dusk, watching the lamplight that glowed in *Trilby's* skylight. He did not care if he waited all night, if Gil did not appear. He supposed Albert had thought he would follow him back on board the *Flower*; good-natured Albert who did not want to suspect, who was even more nervous of looking into Sam's black pit than Sam himself. ' God, make it come next week,' Sam thought, ' and everything all right again. God, make the time pass.' He stuck his chin down into the roll neck of his jersey, and watched *Trilby* closely, his eyes never moving away from her afterdeck. He was picturing Gil sitting on Finch's bunk, lighting a cigarette at the stove, pushing his cap up off his forehead and wiping at the salt and the sweat with the back of his hand. Or was he already stretched out in the second bunk, dozing off?

A dark shape appeared in the hatch, and Sam heard the scutter of a dog's paws on the deck. Gil picked the dog up and threw him on the quay, then grasped the rungs of the ladder and started to climb up after him. Sam backed hurriedly behind a tower of fish-boxes, and watched Gil set off across the quay, Scruff running ahead of him. Gil was not hurrying, but he walked steadily, not aimlessly as if he were just taking Scruff for a run. Painfully, like a physical stab in his flesh, Sam's memory played him a trick by releasing suddenly a dozen pictures of Gil jumping off *Trilby* after a long passage to give Scruff a run: at Ipswich, at Mistley, along the sea-wall at Heybridge and at Battlesbridge, kicking stones along the wharf at Rochford and Colchester. Gil grinning, throwing sticks, careless, not hunched and sullenly threading his way through these sour alien streets. Sam wanted to run after him and stop him, but his feet kept merely walking, following without gaining. The streets were nearly empty; it was cold and the wind was gusting down the narrow alleys. Across the Place d'Armes the lights of 'Chez Jules' were dimmed behind the blinds. The café appeared shut, but Gil went round the corner to the side, opened a door to a back yard and disappeared inside. Sam went on walking, as if his feet did not belong to him, until he arrived on the corner, beside the blank gate. There was nobody about. He leaned his head against the brick wall and said, 'Gil! Oh, Gil!'

He stood there a long time, not knowing what to do. It was Gil, not Bunyard, who was the spy, yet Sam could not believe the evidence of what he had seen. His mind groped for another explanation of Gil's visiting 'Jules', and he remembered Albert saying that Jules might have a daughter Gil was interested in. This poor, vague suggestion was Sam's only crumb of hope. He nourished it, visualizing Gil in the embrace of a beautiful French girl behind the stone wall. He strained his ears for clues, but the wind was creaking the broken shutters at the windows above. Sam could not bear to face the truth of what he had discovered and, set on finding an alibi for Gil, he opened the yard gate and went inside.

The yard was empty. Across a narrow area of paving stones, littered with empty bottles and bins of garbage, chinks of light shone out of the ill-fitting kitchen door and window at the back of the bar. The regulation blinds at the window were askew, and Sam stepped forward to see if he could see inside, but as he did so the door opened without warning, and Jules came out with a crate of empty bottles. Standing in the middle of the yard, Sam had no chance of concealing himself.

Jules dropped the crate with a crash. Sam leapt for the gate, but could not find the latch. He scrabbled for it frantically, but Jules was up to him in two strides. Sam ducked, but Jules caught him by the shoulder and spun him round to face him, and his right fist, doubled and even bigger than Bunyard's, came up with all the man's force into Sam's diaphragm. With the physical blow, Sam knew that his world had truly crumbled. He fell full-length, reeling amongst the noisy bottles, sick and almost unconscious with

the fearful agony in his middle, unable to move, or even breathe. He felt as if his lungs had burst. Choking, he was lifted up by his coat collar and dragged roughly into the house, into a brightness thick with cooking smells and cigarette smoke. Jules dropped him on the scrubbed stone flags, and a torrent of French broke out above him, but Sam was only concerned with trying to draw a breath, gasping

and writhing on the floor like a landed fish. He could not
understand any of the conversation which boomed and
receded in his eardrums. He saw faces floating a long way off,
and Gil's face amongst them, with no expression in it. He
tried to say 'Gil' but could not. Gil said, in English, 'I
do not know him,' and Sam saw his lips frame the words,
and heard the words in his ears, but he did not understand.
Scruff came up to Sam and licked his face, and Sam put a
hand up to his rough fur, but the pain in his diaphragm
stopped him, and he doubled up again with a moan of
despair.

Then there was a long flight of stairs, dimly lit by a gas
lamp. Sam remembered the stairs, the scrape and thump of
each step as he was dragged up into the darkness above, the
journey laced with French invective and grunts and kicks.
The smell of garlic breath was in his nostrils, the soft, angry
French falling in an incessant stream about his head. He did
not know how many men there were, nor who they were,
nor where he was, nor anything save that they dragged him
into a place smelling of mothballs and dust and stale, damp
eiderdowns and wound him into a cocoon of helplessness
with quick, efficient knots. They stuffed his mouth full of
rags so that he could scarcely breathe, let alone cry out, and
bound his arms and ankles and made the ropes fast to a leg
of a big double bed. He tried to protest, to cry out, to get up,
but he could do nothing, and could make no sound. He pulled
frantically at the bedpost but it did not budge, and when
they left him he shouted after them—he screamed at them—
but not a whisper could get through their efficient gag. He
heard a door slam beside him and heavy feet receding
down the stairs. It was suddenly very quiet, and he heard his
own breathing, choking and wheezing through the rags,
like Albert's. 'Albert,' he said silently to the darkness.
'Albert.'

He lay still for a long time, losing track of time. He was

acutely uncomfortable, but his mind was not concerned with physical pain. He kept seeing Gil's face floating towards him, saying, 'I do not know him,' and he kept wondering whether, in his half-consciousness, he had imagined Gil downstairs, and not really seen him there at all. He could not remember where this dreadful nightmare had started; whether it was only with the blow to his stomach, or earlier, when Gil had gone through the gate, or when they had first seen Scruff lying on the floor beneath the bar. The sequence of events was confused. Sam kept seeing *Trilby* reaching in past the pier, and Scruff's sympathetic pink tongue, and Gil's face as he said, 'I do not know him,' but nothing was in any order. It all milled through his head, shuffled, inconsequent and unreal. He rolled against the ropes, pushing with his feet against the wall, but the bed shifted only an inch. His arms were beginning to go numb and he knew he would never get free of his own accord.

Slowly, as his head cleared and the hours slipped past, the full significance of his predicament came home to him. The more painful his physical circumstances grew with the passing of time, the more sharply he realized his own danger. At two o'clock the *Flower of Ipswich* would sail without him. If Albert knew where he was, he was unlikely to be able to do anything about it and Sam thought rescue could be discounted. Which brought him for the first time to the disquieting question: what was Jules intending to do with him? Sam rolled miserably against the bedpost, staring towards the faint light that came in through a window across the room. He did not think Jules intended him to sail on the *Flower* again, next tide or any other. He had found out—more through Jules's own alarm than through anything he had seen—that Jules was a spy, and that Gil was a messenger for him. He could not see that their actions could mean anything else. Lying there, it was all now very clear and very bleak in his mind, accepted and understood. He thought if he could accept that, there was nothing else ever likely to happen to him that could approach this fact for rock-bottom bitterness. He could not bear to think of Gil: Gil's reddish, diffident face with the quiet, soft eyes, Gil's way with the devoted Scruff. Gil last summer. Before Agnes. 'It's her,' Sam thought. 'It's Agnes who has unhinged him. He's gone mad.' He rolled over again, feeling sick. If he were sick he would choke and die, he thought, but the pain had come back into his chest, making him feel sick. And then he thought, 'But Jules is going to kill me, so what difference is it going to make?' and he lay there trying to make sense of this idea. But, even if Gil was a spy, Sam could not accept that he himself was going to die. He did not know what was going to happen, but he was determined not to die. Not now, at least.

But the long hours in the darkness with his bitter truths tried him to the very end of his tether. He had never supposed he was very brave, and he tried to think of the British soldiers, not far away, who according to his weekly magazine were the quintessence of courage. He tried to lie there bravely like a British soldier, but he knew in his heart that they were as frightened as he was now. 'But it's not cowardly to be frightened,' he remembered, 'only if because of fright you don't do the right thing.' And he had no choice now about doing the right thing or the wrong, for he was as helpless as a chicken. He could not scream or beat his breast in despair, or run away. He rolled about, trying to ease the cramps and pains, and pretended he was being brave, because he wasn't screaming. It was better to think about that than about Gil.

The house was old and heavily-built, and it was difficult to hear what was going on, but Sam thought he heard some women talking in another bedroom, and presumed that, in spite of the alarms of the evening, they were going to bed as usual. Would Jules be going fishing as usual? Sam, in such an unusual situation himself, was appalled by the thought that life could be going on for his captor as if nothing had happened. Was he going to be left tied to the bedpost for ever? He thought of the *Flower* sailing, Bunyard cursing his absence. . . . He heaved on the bedpost but the pain in his chest stabbed him. ' He's broken my ribs,' he thought, but it did not seem to matter beside the other things. He kicked the wall, and smelt the damp plaster as it flaked down. He thumped and banged on the floor, but it took all his little remaining strength and breath. When he lay still again the pains coursed down his arms and legs, stirred by his activity.

Some time later—he had no way of telling how long—he heard a floorboard creak under his ear. He listened intently and felt, rather than heard, someone moving not far away. Moving very quietly. A door handle turned. Sam twisted round, staring into the darkness, feeling his own muffled breath beating in his throat. Somebody was there, but he could not see anything, only feel this presence. The floorboard moved under his ear again. Sam rolled over, thumping the wall, and a voice whispered, ' Sam? '

Sam felt the hands on him, exploring up over his neck and down his arms. He felt himself trembling, and the hard, rough fingers pulling at the knots of his gag.

' Don't say anything.'

The fumbling seemed to take a century. Sam choked in anticipation, spitting and moaning as the foul mouthful of dirty rags came away, feeling his breath surge with a wonderful freedom that for a moment put all other thoughts out of his head.

' Gil! '

' Hush. Don't make a noise.'

A knife was working on the ropes now, slicing through the turns. Sam lay taking great breaths, a relief surging through him that, for a few minutes, almost amounted to happiness. When at last he could move his arms, the agony of it was a delight he knew he could bear. He sat up, stretching and wincing, almost sobbing with relief. Gil sat on the bed and rubbed Sam's shoulders and wrists to get the life back into them, his big hands gentle. He did not say anything, and in the darkness Sam could not see his face. When at last Sam was able to stand, Gil did not move.

' You must go,' he whispered to Sam. ' I can't do any more.'

' Go? How? '

' Down the stairs and out through the kitchen. The door is unlocked. All the women are in bed and asleep and the men have gone. You will just catch the *Flower* in time.'

' What are you going to do? '

' I don't know. Get along.'

' Gil— '

' Get along. Don't speak to me.'

Sam hesitated. He wanted Gil to come with him, but Gil sat on the bed with his head buried in his hands. Then Sam thought of the *Flower* ready to sail, and the fear of missing her prodded him into life again. The thought of her, the familiar forepeak, the damp mattress, the wheeze of Albert's breathing near by—she was the most desirable thing in the world. She was home and everything he knew, and Bunyard's stooped figure was the essence of comfort and security. Without another word, Sam limped to the door and went out of the room.

The darkness outside the door was complete. Sam was terrified. From somewhere he could hear a woman snoring, from under his foot a board creaked. He put out his hands, groping blindly, and after a few wild sweeps he found a banister rail. The snoring continued as Sam patted his way desperately down a narrow landing. His own breathing was almost as loud as the snoring, his feet, clumsy and numb like skittles, stumbling in the ragged matting. The darkness and the dank smell of the French house suffocated him. ' Oh,

God, get me out of here,' he prayed. ' Please get me down these ruddy stairs.'

The boards groaned and the plaster flaked under his fingers as he crept down towards the kitchen. At the bottom of the stairs he was in a black well, and could find no way out. Sweating and in despair, he groped and shuffled, fear mounting, impatience pushing him to indiscretion. A door-frame was there, a door latch, and beyond its noisy clatter a square of half-light, a window. He could smell the warm cinders of a fire.

' It's the kitchen,' he thought.

Eagerly he stepped forward, and caught his knee against something unexpected, and ill-balanced. What it was he never knew, but it was something that shattered to fragments on the stone flags, with a ringing like the church bells of all Calais. Upstairs, someone screamed. Sam heard the ceiling above him shudder, a door open, and a torrent of excitement take up the echoes still resounding in the kitchen. Calm now, with the situation rapidly getting out of control, Sam made for the window and flung up the sash. He went out of the window as somebody came in at the door behind him. How many women there were in ' Chez Jules ', Sam was in no situation to discover, but the one, two or three of them put up a pandemonium he was never to hear equalled.

He crossed the yard and found the yard gate open. He went out into the street and started to run, drunkenly, the pain in his side like a flame under his ribs. The dark, rain-skinned streets echoed to the screams behind him, a man bawled, window sashes flew up with hollow rattles in all directions. The Jules's women were behind him in long flannel nightdresses and flying plaits, screaming as they ran, and all the secret night life of Calais: the drunks, the lovers, the lost and the wanderers, were drawn to the excitement like moths to a flame. Faces ran out of every alley. A man clutched at Sam's arm, and Sam swerved and ran on. The voices

screamed after him. He was a thief, a Boche, a murderer.
Sam was appalled and terrified, his strength failing him, his
boots sliding and skidding on the cobbles. He had never
dreamed of anything like this. White-faced, gasping, he
felt the rain hit him as he came out on to the quays, the
coldness of the sea wind on the fire of his panic, and he
thought of it in the *Flower's* sails and leapt frantically down
the quay.

The lock gates were open. Moving slowly to the throb of
her powerful engine the *Notre Dame de Calais* was just
moving through the gates. The men on the warps above her
turned round as Sam pounded past but could not leave their
work in the strong wind. Their voices roared after him,
laughing at his flight, but shrilly above them, distant but
piercing, Sam heard the alarm of the approaching Jules's
women. The breath had not deserted their capacious bosoms;
they were indefatigable, strong as Flanders nags under the
home-made lace, and they were out to stop Sam.

'They will tell Jules!' Sam knew that if the *Flower* were
gone he was doomed. Jules was there, at the wheel of the

Notre Dame, steering her into the lock, and he knew the importance of Sam. Sam had no strength and no hope left. He ran blindly, desperate and despairing, and saw through the glaze of his exhaustion a black topsail moving beyond the lock gates. It moved inexorably, hard to the fresh wind. Sam ran faster. He shouted, ' Mr. Bunyard! Mr. Bunyard! ' but it came out a cry of despair, his lungs bursting. The topsail moved on, slipping away faster, but Sam was past the lock and running down the side of the basin where the *Flower* was beginning to bear away for the close-hauled reach out to sea. Sam saw the mainsail brails break out and the great curtain of black canvas drop down. He stopped and screamed, ' Mr. Bunyard! '

The *Flower of Ipswich*, instead of going about to make out to sea, freed off and swooped towards the quayside. Sam saw Bunyard turning round, swearing, the wheel already spinning to take the barge off again. Sam had a split second to jump as the big transom swung in towards the wall, and he launched himself spread-eagled from the quayside. Even in mid-air he heard the Jules's women's vituperation following, and he thought that even if he missed the barge the black waters of the harbour would be more welcome than the embrace of their sinewy arms.

With one hand he caught the corner of the transom. All the remaining strength in his body flowed into the grip of his one hand, which held him, dangling and kicking, above the water, until Albert ran down the deck and heaved him on board.

6 'La Notre Dame de Calais'

In the few minutes that he lay on deck recovering, only one
fact had any meaning in Sam's head. He held on to it
frantically, through the black pain that enmeshed him:
nobody must know what had happened. What he had
found out. Not Albert, not Bunyard, nor anybody else in
the world.

Fortunately Bunyard and Albert were fully occupied with
sailing the barge out of the harbour, and had no time to

attend to Sam, so that by the time the *Flower of Ipswich* was
out between the piers and crashing into the big seas outside,
Sam had had several minutes in which to recover. He raised
himself painfully on to his elbows and looked out over the
bulwarks, and saw a stormbound moon rolling over the
ragged clouds, silvering the wide white beaches of the
Calais shore where the wind was blowing the sand in long
lines off the dunes. The loom of the lighthouse flared inter-
mittently, needling the wild sea. Sam thought of Gil sitting
on the bed with his face in his hands. He thought, 'Perhaps
there is a mistake somewhere. Perhaps it isn't true.'

The *Flower of Ipswich* was on course to clear the South
Goodwin, stemming the ebb tide with a strong southerly on
her quarter. Bunyard was at the wheel and Albert was
stowing warps. Bunyard had not so much as cast a glance
or a word in Sam's direction, but Sam did not delude himself
that the incident was going to be overlooked. He got to his
feet and went below for his smock, staggering along the
heaving deck. Albert followed him, avid with curiosity.

'What happened? Where've you been?'

'Nothing. Nowhere. Don't ask me,' Sam muttered.

'What's wrong with you?'

'Nothing. I'm not telling you anything,' Sam said. 'I'm
not telling anybody anything.'

He pulled his heavy smock over his head to close the
conversation, grateful for the respite. He turned his back on
Albert, and emerged with his face turned doggedly towards
the companion-way. Pulling his cap down hard, he started
to climb back on deck.

'But where've you been?' Albert insisted. 'You'll have
to tell the old man.'

It was blowing too hard on deck to carry on a conversation
without shouting, so Sam took advantage of the fact and
made his way aft in silence. Bunyard said, 'You can take
the wheel, now you've decided to join us.'

Sam grasped the spokes reluctantly. In heavy weather Bunyard usually took the wheel himself, but now he stepped back behind Sam and stood with his hands in his pockets, watching the sails.

' West sou'-west,' Bunyard said.

' West sou'-west,' Sam muttered.

Bunyard growled something to Albert, and Albert came up to help Sam as lee helmsman. Sam, with the pain still kicking in his ribs, was glad of Albert's help, as the barge was bearing up into the wind like a wayward horse and had to be continually corrected. She was carrying reefed main and staysail and crashing into the big seas, shouldering them over her decks in fountains of white spray. There was not a moment for Sam's mind to wander. He was completely occupied with the telltale swing of the compass needle, and all the remainder of his energy was required to hold the barge on her mad course. The agonies of the last few hours were dissolved in the roar of water under the *Flower's* leeboard, and in the creaking and straining of the gear aloft. Already Sam could feel the salt on his face and the spray clammy round his neck; already he was swearing at the old barge, as they always did when she almost pulled their arms out of their sockets.

' Strewth! ' Albert muttered. ' Hold the old gal! I reckon the navy'd be a rest-cure after the *Flower*! '

Sam even laughed.

The full moon reared above the topmast. The *Flower's* decks gleamed like palace floors and the spray came down in a cascade of diamonds.

' Cor blimey! It's ruddy beautiful,' Albert said.

' Ruddy beautiful for U-boats,' Sam commented.

' Yes, but them old Zeppelins'd be over China the minute they left the ground. So we're all right that way.'

Zeppelins were the peril of clear, windless nights, U-boats the menace of the full moon. Sam looked round anxiously from time to time when he had the chance, but saw nothing more ominous than a trawler astern. U-boats did not set a gaff sail.

' If that's a Froggie, he's coming a long way out,' Albert remarked. He stood watching, and Bunyard turned round and looked too.

' Steam trawler,' Bunyard remarked. 'The *Notre Dame de Calais*, if I'm any judge.'

Sam, concentrating on the wheel, felt as if someone had laid a cold hand on his stomach. He lifted his eyes from the compass and saw a puzzled expression pass over Albert's face. Albert looked at him and raised his eyebrows. Sam felt as if he had been hit between the eyes.

' Funny, her coming out here,' Albert said.

Sam bit his lip. She had a two-pounder in her bows, he remembered. Old British barges like the *Flower of Ipswich* foundered regularly in such seas, and who was to know that a shell from a two-pound gun had not helped one of them on her way? His scalp prickled under his damp cap. Why else would she be following them, after the events of the previous evening?

' Any connexion? ' Albert wheezed in his ear, as if reading his thoughts. 'I mean—your night out and her—? ' He jerked his head to indicate the trawler.

A great spasm of fear seemed to burst in Sam's throat. He thought his adventure was finished, not merely starting.

' He's out to get us! ' he whispered hoarsely to Albert as they heaved on the wheel together. 'He's not out fishing, that's for sure! '

' Not out here, mate,' Albert agreed. He paused. 'Bags you tell the old man,' he added.

' Are you ruddy joking? ' Sam whispered, near to tears. All the strength he had gathered for the job at the wheel seemed to have deserted him. He was shivering, and ravenous

with hunger. He glanced behind and saw Bunyard, unper-
turbed, looking up at the swaying sprit and the moon
floating above it, a monstrous bob at the masthead.

'You think he's goin' to catch us up, sir?' Albert said to
him.

'Who catch us up?'

'That Froggie steam trawler.'

Bunyard turned round and stared out over the stern.
Albert gave Sam a nudge that nearly knocked him over.
'I reckon he's beating us,' he said to Bunyard.

'What, a Frog fisherman?' Bunyard said scornfully. He
stared intently at the boat behind them. Smoke was shredding
from the lips of her narrow funnel, and all her brand-new
canvas was set, from bowsprit to mizzen.

'What's he in such a hurry for then?' Bunyard muttered.

'Making a race of it, I reckon,' Albert said with a great
show of nonchalance.

Bunyard was obviously interested. He said nothing, but
turned round at intervals to keep an eye on the trawler. Sam
concentrated on keeping the *Flower* on course, trying to
convince himself that the presence of the *Notre Dame* was
mere coincidence. But those dreadful women were aboard
her—of that he felt sure. Screaming at Jules as he stood at the
wheel, their big bosoms heaving still with the chase. They
haunted Sam, and he was too tired to think logically any
more. Albert nudged him again, his face agleam with cunning,
but Sam was past caring.

'Wind's easing,' Bunyard said, very non-committally.
'Let go the lower brails, Albert. She'll carry all her sail
now.'

'It's worked!' Albert whispered to Sam in triumph, as
Bunyard turned round to stare astern once more. 'He's
going to make a race of it!'

'But she's a steamer,' Sam said. 'He's mad.' Bunyard
didn't know how badly the *Notre Dame* wanted him. If

Jules had decided that he was going to get the *Flower*, the mere shaking out of a reef was not going to make much difference. Sam wished he could think straight, but he was past it now. Bunyard said to him, ' Go and help Albert,' and stepped forward to take the wheel. Sam scrambled to the brail winch and took the handle off Albert.

' The wind's not eased really,' Albert said eagerly. ' But he can't bear being beaten. I knew it would work ! '

Sam was too frightened to say anything. Didn't Albert remember the two-pounder? Or didn't he think Jules was in earnest? He let go the brails and watched the great black folds of the mainsail crack out into the wind. The *Flower* surged into a wave and threw a sheet of water over them. The sea roared through the lee scuppers with a noise like the gun Sam was thinking about. The spray ran down his face and he groaned softly, appalled at his own imaginings. The moon was shining mercilessly, and beyond the rearing shape of the mizzen sail he saw the *Notre Dame de Calais* sharply drawn against the glittering sea. She was sailing hard and steaming too, the propeller driving her through the big waves when the sails would have let her ride them. She would be even wetter aboard than the *Flower*. Sam pictured Jules at the wheel, and hoped desperately that he had the women aboard with him, and that they were being sick, desperately, despairingly sick. . . .

' Did Gil go there, then? ' Albert was saying.

' No,' said Sam roughly. ' He didn't. But I did instead, and that's all I'm saying, so shut up about it.'

' Wait till he fires that gun,' he was thinking. He was frightened, and not even ashamed of it. What if they all got killed, because of Gil? Not just himself, but Bunyard and Albert too, who did not even know what was happening. Sam went back to the wheel to help Bunyard, and the water came running up the deck, swirling round his ankles. The *Flower* was travelling as fast as he had ever known her, but it took all their combined strength to hold her on course, and in the struggle Sam had no time to think about anything else. Albert stood braced against the mizzen stay, reporting progress.

' I reckon we're holding him,' he remarked.

' We keep this up, and it'll be our fastest passage since Christmas,' Bunyard said, with some satisfaction. He looked up at the bare, swaying topmast. ' Be light soon. We'll be off Deal for breakfast.'

Surely Jules would not follow them to England? Sam had no chance to look behind, but he could see the sky paling, the moon's brilliance failing as the long June day started on the Eastern horizon. June! Sam thought bitterly. It was true that the wind was easing slightly, and that by evening the Channel might be as sweet as a poem, but the last six hours in Sam's opinion had been as dark a hell as any he could remember. Over the thunder of the barge's way, another crash shook the air. Sam felt the shock in his eardrums, and knew instantly what it was. Albert looked round in amazement.

' What—? '

' Firing,' said Bunyard.

' Who's firing? '

' It's not a sea-gull.'

' It's—! ' Albert was incoherent with astonishment. He looked at Sam, but Sam would not meet his eyes. Another explosion shivered the deck planks under their feet, and Bunyard started to swear.

' Who does he think we are? A ruddy Fritz? '

' But he *knows* who we are! ' Albert said.

' Perhaps that's why he's firing then,' Bunyard said shortly. ' You had anything to do with that Frog? ' he asked Sam. ' Been meddling? '

Sam pressed his lips tight together and shook his head.

' My God, I'll report him when we get in. I'll see he doesn't get away with this, the spying, treacherous devil.'

Bunyard was goaded in mid-sentence by another salvo that broke close enough to stun their ears. Sam felt the shock of the explosion in the water come up through the deck into the soles of his feet, but the *Flower* plunged on like a great galloping horse, and they could do nothing but hold the wheel to stop her bearing up. Sam turned round and put his back to it, his hands locked under one of the spokes, and the pain in his ribs racking him, making him gasp. ' All right, sink, you old wreck! ' his mind was saying to her. ' Nothing worse can happen! If I get blown up I won't have anything to worry about any more.' The phrase ' under fire ' ran through his head. So this was it! The magic phrase of *The War Illustrated*, that conjured up visions of glory. And Sam knew he was afraid.

The next shell was so close that they heard it whine before it exploded in the sea off their quarter. Albert, one hand on the mizzen stay, did a little step-dance and chanted the familiar bars: ' Hush, here comes a whizz-bang! '

' It's getting light,' Sam thought. It might save them. Soon they would see, as they had seen so many times before, the thin sunlight picking out the white cliffs of Kent, and then— surely—the *Notre Dame de Calais* would turn back? ' He's not crazy,' Sam thought. ' He'll only sink us if he thinks he can do it without being discovered.' Or was he crazy? The whole world, at that moment, seemed crazy to Sam. Sweat ran down his face, with the effort of holding the wheel, and he watched the fading stars skimming above the sprit, and prayed for the daylight.

' . . . and it's making straight for me! ' sang Albert.

There was more truth in the song than he knew. Sam felt as if someone had picked him up bodily and flung him across the deck. His ears seemed to crack right into the middle of his head and his eyes exploded. His ribs cried out with pain. 'Oh, it's happened! It's happened! ' and he was rolling into the scuppers, to be brought up sharp against the shrouds.

Immediately, because the sail was still standing above him, the big sprit holding it against the sky, he thought, ' It's not too bad. We're not dismasted,' and he rolled to his feet.

Albert was lying by the wheel, making a strange choking noise, and the wheel was spinning over his head. Bunyard was sprawled over the skylight, but already cursing and struggling to his feet. Curiously, the after part of the barge looked strangely bare, and it took Sam a few seconds, in his dazed condition, to realize that the mizzen-mast had disappeared. It had gone over the side, and the *Flower* was trailing it behind her, a tangle of ripped sail and rigging, like a disembowelment. The crippled barge, unattended, was plunging in the eye of the wind, rattling blocks and sheets with heavy, jarring thuds.

' Get her sailing! ' Bunyard snapped to Sam.

The mainsail was flogging, the block crashing madly along the horse close by Albert's head. Bunyard stooped and dragged Albert roughly out of the way, and Sam started to push the wheel up, but the rudder was fouled with all the broken mizzen and after half a turn he could not move it any more. He held the wheel with his body, and Bunyard said, ' Lock it then, and help me.' Sam put the lock on the wheel, stumbled over Albert and started to heave on the tangled rigging.

' Wait, wait.' Bunyard had his knife out to deal with the sheets, but the wire rigging was an impenetrable tangle.

' We'll have to get it all inboard. It's the boom that's fouling the rudder. Here . . .' Struggling, cursing, but agile as a monkey, the old man got a hold on the splintered spar and started dragging it aboard. Together, swearing, slipping, and in a nightmare of fear for the next explosion, they cleared the rudder. Sam went back to the wheel and was able to get the *Flower* back on course, and Bunyard told him to stay there and sail like hell while he set about getting all the hampering wreckage on board. ' Like hell,' Sam agreed, his ears pricking for the next shrill whine, his sticky hands gripping the stubborn spokes. He glanced at Albert, hearing him moan, and saw a trickle of blood run down over his jaw from underneath his cap.

' Albert! ' Unable to help him, he stirred him gently with his foot, and Albert muttered something, and turned his head.

' You all right? '

But the wheel demanded all his attention. He had to ease her as the big waves reared under her bows, and pull her back on course, ease her and correct her and keep her moving at her wild ten knots towards the daylight and the line of white cliffs which spelt safety. The sky was pale now and full of the luminous promise of sun, but the *Flower of Ipswich* was a cripple and their lucky shot had inspired the Frenchmen. The crump of the two-pounder rang in Sam's ears, and waiting for the next one was worse: the thud and the cringe, waiting to see the mast come down or a hole blown in her side. Sam's heart seemed to be thumping inside his head, loud as the two-pounder. Without the black shape of the mizzen sail behind him, and the trunk of her mast, he felt horribly vulnerable, standing up on the naked stern fully exposed to the range of Jules's gun. He kept looking at Albert, wanting to do something for him, but he couldn't. Albert's eyes were open, but the blood was still running down his cheek.

Another shell exploded in the water close beside the *Flower's* bows and she shuddered. Sam both heard and felt the thud of the shell splinters in her planking.

' Two-inch oak,' he thought. ' Old Jules'll want a direct hit to make a hole in her. Try again, you ruddy Frog! '

Above his head the big mainsail, hard with wind, swayed against the dawn sky. She was lovely, Sam thought, with a fierce exhilaration. There was nothing more to shock and frighten: nothing worse could happen, when Jules had split her open and they were drowned—and he was filled with this fierce, strange defiance that overcame fear.

' Go on ! ' he thought. ' Sink her if you can ! '

He had been afraid so much that night, there was suddenly no fear left in him. Turning briefly, he saw the *Notre Dame* half a mile astern, outlined against the first light of the sun. The sea was bright, a hard green marbled with the moving crests of breaking waves, as splendid a dawn sea as he had ever laid eyes on. The light that he had prayed for was making the *Flower* an easier target for the French trawler and, even with the Kentish coast looming up, her spires of chalk milky against the greenish sky, Jules was still coming.

' He can smell blood,' Sam thought.

Two more shells whistled overhead and exploded ahead of them. Sam turned round to see how Bunyard was getting on, and the old man looked up.

' Going nicely,' Bunyard said. ' I'll be with you in a minute.'

Surrounded by the wreck of the mizzen-mast, he gave Sam a grim smile. ' That old naval patrol,' he commented. ' Always around when we don't want 'em. But when we do—!' He shook his head. ' Drinkin' tea off Deal pier,' he said.

They both heard the next shell keening out of the sun, and ducked together. The barge heeled to meet it on the crest of a breaking wave, and the spray burst over them as the shell hit the foredeck. Sam clung to the wheel, his head between his arms, and the blast and the spray and the splinters all came together, almost rocking him off his feet. The wheel heaved beneath him, and instinctively he was correcting it, still sailing her, although when he looked forward again the staysail was flogging loose, in tatters, and there was a hole in the foredeck big enough to jump through.

' Up helm ! ' Bunyard was beside him, thrusting at the wheel. ' Run her before it ! Easy does it. Easy.'

They steadied the wheel between them so that the barge changed course to run before the wind, at right-angles to her former course. This brought her broadside on to the *Notre Dame de Calais*, and Sam thought it would all be over very shortly. But there was too much to do to think about the next shell.

' He's shortened sail for us, saved us a job,' Bunyard said. ' I don't like the look of that forestay. Hold her like this, watch you don't gybe.'

Running, the barge rode the seas and the waves no longer broke over her deck. With the hole in her, she would have to be kept dry. Sam watched Bunyard working up forward, as if he had all the time in the world, as if the next screaming shell were meant for somebody else a hundred miles away. Running, the barge surged along, lifting herself over the big waves with an easy, rolling motion, but the *Notre Dame de Calais* was now quite close on her quarter. Sam could even make out the muzzle of her gun over the bows. The *Flower* was a sitting target, her long flank exposed. The loss of mizzen and staysail had slowed her down considerably, but the hole in her deck was more dangerous than the loss of sail. If there were any planks stove in below it, she would soon be under. Sam knew all this, and thought of it with a detachment that surprised him. It was not right, he was thinking, to be drowned on such a lovely morning.

' Sam.'

' You all right? ' Sam said.

Albert was lifting himself on one elbow, exploring his bloody head gingerly with one hand.

' Listen,' Albert said.

' You all right? '

' A queer noise,' Albert said.

' It's your head,' Sam said. But there was a noise. Sam heard it too. Not the screaming of a shell, but an engine noise, in the sky. Sam looked up, but could see nothing beyond the bellying mainsail.

' What is it? ' he shouted to Bunyard, who was standing

with a hand on the forestay, looking up doubtfully. Bunyard
pointed. There was a sudden roar, almost a clatter, and Sam
jumped as from behind the sprit an aeroplane materialized as
if from nowhere. He had a glimpse of the wheels almost
brushing the mast-top; he saw the intricate wirework
between the wings all picked out with the sun, the spinning
propeller, the pilot leaning over staring at them, shouting
something, gesticulating. On the top of the wings a gun was
mounted. Sam saw every detail quite plainly, from the
roundels painted on the fuselage to the excitement in the
pilot's eyes behind his goggles. Bunyard was coming back
down the deck, almost running. The plane zoomed away,
gaining height, the wind whining in its stays, and Bunyard
came to Sam at the wheel and said, ' Perhaps it will be all
right. Watch you don't gybe her. Watch her.'

Sam tore his eyes away from the plane to watch his course,
then, hypnotized, watched the aeroplane again. It was
against the sun, a glittering, delicate, deadly machine seeming
to hover like a hawk over the French trawler. Bunyard's eyes
were lit up like a boy's.

' That'll stop him! That'll show 'im! Give it to him,
the—' He called Jules all the names he could think of,
standing beside Sam at the wheel. They heard the staccato
clatter of the Lewis gun as the plane dived, and Sam saw the
Notre Dame de Calais change course abruptly, sails flogging.
' The helmsman's busy saving his own skin,' Bunyard said.

The plane pulled out of its dive over the trawler's topmast
and climbed steeply, banking and climbing so that the
sun outlined its wings in gold. It was to Sam the loveliest
sight he had ever seen, and he gazed after it, full of a heady
gratitude. He felt warm and human again, and full of a
strange tenderness for everything about him, which now he
was not to lose. He felt like crying. The dark red mainsail of
the *Notre Dame* was ripped with bullets and was blowing out
in long ribbons from the gaff. She was changing course, the

helmsman back at the wheel, steaming round in a big circle
to make for home. The plane was circling over it, the pilot
peering curiously out of the cockpit, obviously puzzled by
what had been going on. But as the *Notre Dame* steamed for
Calais, the aeroplane came back, circled once over the *Flower*
and then, receiving the thumbs-up signal from Bunyard,
soared up again into the bright sky and made off towards
the coast.

7 Gil Comes Home

Afterwards, it was Albert whom Sam remembered most vividly when his mind went back to the incident: Albert lying in Bunyard's bunk with his black hair all clotted with blood, and a strange, absent expression in his eyes. They had had little opportunity to do much for him, save put him in the bunk, and when they had anchored in Dover a naval launch had taken him ashore to hospital. Since then, Sam had heard nothing of him. He had helped Bunyard tidy up the crippled barge and nail up the hole in the deck, then, acting on orders from the Guv'nor in London, they had sailed the *Flower* up to Ipswich for repairs. The yard manager said a week for the job, and Sam went home.

If Sam had gone home unwillingly before, it was as nothing to the reluctance with which he set off for Fambridge this time. The last time he had been with Gil. This time he was alone, but Gil dominated his mind more surely than if he had been there in person. Sam kept seeing Albert all covered with blood, and his dull, wandering eyes, and he kept thinking, ' Gil did it. It is because of Gil.' What had happened to Albert epitomized what Gil's crime was all about: to be a spy was to kill people like Albert and Manny. Sam could not see that it was anything less.

' If I hadn't gone to Jules,' he thought, ' Albert would be all right.' But if he hadn't gone to Jules, Jules would still be a spy and so would Gil, whereas Jules was now in trouble with the authorities (Bunyard having reported the incident) and no doubt too frightened to carry on with his treachery, and Gil . . . At this point Sam's imagination failed.

What was Gil doing? What was Gil thinking? Sam, appalled, could not begin to find an excuse for Gil. He had

lied for Gil, to Bunyard and to Albert; he had told no one of
what he had discovered the night he followed Gil. He had
nursed his bitter knowledge to himself, and the burden of it
was unbearable. His silence was more through shame than
loyalty; to admit that a Goodchild could be a traitor to his
country was more than Sam could manage, and the shame
of it suffused every minute of his day, and filled his dreams
at night. And to keep Gil's secret, he realized, was to connive
in the spying, so that he was guilty too. All the time that Gil
was protected, so Gil's work could be killing British soldiers
in France. The enormity of Gil's crime crushed Sam completely. He knew spies were shot. If he were to tell anyone—
Bunyard, for instance—he thought Gil would be shot. And
if he were to keep the knowledge to himself, Manny instead
might be shot, and a thousand others like him.

Sitting in the train on his way home, pressed against a
crowd of cheerful, sweating humanity, Sam thought his
dilemma would split his mind in two. He had discovered,
in the last few weeks, that he had not as much courage as he
had hoped; that he had no great confidence in his own
judgement. Yet his problem could not be shared. His forehead pressed against the train window, he saw the young
cornfields passing, and placid cows browsing by winding,
reedy streams, and farm wagons jolting along the warm
lanes, and he wondered if this unfamiliar countryside knew
that there was a war on. Bloody, dull-eyed Albert was
unknown here, and the grey thumping of the guns beyond
Calais. Sam felt alien. Although he considered himself a
civilian, amongst these comfortable travellers he felt a
veteran. He had been ' under fire '; they had not budged
from the comforts of home life. In fact, they had prospered.
While the volunteers were being shot down in the trenches,
the men who stayed at home were earning more money
than they had ever earned. Sam scowled.

' Cheer up, son, you'll soon be dead,' a man said to him.

Sam thought, ' Albert might be dead now, for all I know.'

He got off the train at Witham, begged himself a lift in a furniture cart to Maldon and walked the rest of the way. He was not in a hurry, and had no wish to look his mother in the eyes any sooner than he need. Fierce battles were raging in France, at Ypres and Aubers Ridge, and her mind would be all for Manny. ' Oh, Manny!' Sam thought, with a great turn-over of longing. 'If only *he* were on one of the barges still!' Manny would know what to do. Sam kicked stones along the road, and watched them skim into the white lace of the cow parsley that filled the verges.

It was a long, dusty walk. The lanes were lush and green, the sky full of the whirring of larks. Several pony traps passed him at a smart pace, but he did not want a lift. He did not want to talk.

' Fat farmers,' he said to himself. ' Getting rich on war.'

He went down the dead-end lane into North Fambridge, and smelt the sour tang of the saltings again as the breeze blew up from the river. He did not want to meet anyone, but just before he got to his mother's cottage he heard hooves clattering on the road behind him. A woman's voice said sharply, ' Oh, stop! It's Sam!' and a sweating cob pulled up with a jerk on its haunches right beside him. Looking down from her perch in the trap was Agnes Martin. Beside her, handling the reins with a bravado the cob did not seem to be appreciating, was a very smart young man in pigskin gloves, with smooth well-greased hair and a black moustache. Sam recognized him as George Young, a contemporary of Manny's who had been a butcher's errand boy when Manny was a barge skipper, but who was now a foreman in a factory in Chelmsford.

' Why, Sam! Where's your barge then? In the river?'

Sam glowered at Agnes. She had her arm tucked under George's, and she was looking down, smiling and dimpling, with this radiance about her that Sam had recognized before.

She wore a wide hat with roses round the brim, and there were pearls and lace round her neck. Her dress was of a shining stuff that looked to Sam very un-villagelike. Beneath her skirt he saw her feet in elegant kid boots, with tiny buttons right up the sides, much too delicate to be cheap. If he had not despised her so, he would have been very impressed.

He thought, ' She's got that red stuff on her lips.' Albert had several good words for girls like her. He looked at her coldly and said, ' She's in Ipswich for repairs.'

' Oh, again? ' said Agnes. ' I thought you were in France.'

Sam hesitated. He looked at George Young, and said carelessly, ' She was shelled. She lost her mizzen, and my mate's in hospital.'

' Oh! ' Agnes's eyes opened wide. She looked at him with an expression of awed delight, while George Young frowned and picked up the whip.

' Wait a minute, George,' Agnes said, holding his arm.

But Sam, despising himself as well as her, started to walk up the path to his home.

'Is Gil in Ipswich too?' Agnes called after him.

'No,' Sam said.

'Is he coming home soon?'

'I don't know.'

Sam pushed open the door and banged angrily into the kitchen. His mother was standing by the fire, waiting for the iron to hot up on the hob. The kitchen was full of laundry and the smell of starch and the big table was piled with ironing.

'*Sam!*'

His mother jumped round, her face twitching with astonishment. She looked very small to Sam, like a little black beetle, her skirts shiny with wear—not, like Agnes's, with affluence—her hair much greyer than he remembered. She ran up and hugged him, and burst into tears, and he had to bend down to kiss her, which he couldn't remember doing before.

' Oh, Sam! Sam! Why didn't you tell me you were coming? '

In her excitement, Sam decided to forget his troubles and bask in his homecoming while he had the opportunity. It was impossible to resist his mother's fussing and pampering: the kettle was already humming, and her laundress's eyes were glinting at the disreputable clothes he had on his back. She chattered nineteen to the dozen, firing questions without waiting for the answers, so that he could sit back and let it all roll over him, pleasant and warm and nothing to do. She cleared the table and plied him with tea and new-baked bread, and gave him Manny's letters to read, and fetched the tin bath, set it in front of the fire and filled it with hot water.

' Just like your father,' she said, holding up his tattered jersey, thick with sweat and salt. ' Wear 'em till they rot. Manny was the only one who looked after himself properly, God bless him. I only hope he's managing all right now. If I wash these, Sam, they'll fall to pieces.' She was dangling his trousers up and down by the legs, so that the pockets rained bits of shackles and lashing and Calais centimes.

' There's a purse in the back pocket. Don't wash that.'

' Just like you. A purse full of money, and you wear tatters like these—'

' The money's for you.'

' Oh, Sam, you're a daft lad.' She counted the money carefully and put it in a vase on the mantelpiece. ' Is this the first bath you've had since the last time you were home? '

' Had plenty o' baths of sea-water. You just stand there often enough, and you get a bath whether you want it or not.'

' Oh, I don't know what's the attraction of these barges! You could get something better, I'd have thought. With your brains.'

' What makes you think you don't need brains on a barge? ' Sam said. He thought of Gil bringing *Trilby* up to the buoys, like gentling a spirited horse to a halt on a sixpence. He sat in the bath looking at his hands which had palms on them that looked as if they were made of leather, the nails all blunted and broken, the joints scarred with winter sores. He remembered George Young's cissy gloves.

' Oh, Sam! Mercy on us! Whatever have you done to your chest? ' His mother dropped his trousers and stared at him, one hand up to her face in horror. Sam, who had never thought to look for any external evidence of Jules's fist, looked down, startled, to find his diaphragm wreathed in purple and green and yellow, like a lurid sunset in oils.

' I fell on the winch,' he muttered.

If only she'd seen him, he thought! All tied up under the bed, and Gil sitting there, with his head in his hands.

' You might have broken a rib! I've got some liniment in the cupboard, when you've finished. My, but it's a real bruise, that one. Come on, don't just sit there. Get washed. I'll find you a shirt. I don't suppose your old ones will fit you any more. Perhaps one of Gil's—'

Fuss, fuss, Sam thought. It warmed him, amongst all his troubles to be fussed over. He got dressed in clean, stiff clothes, and combed his hair and oiled it down flat on his head so that he looked like Albert.

' That's better,' said his mother.

' What difference does it make? ' Sam thought. ' I am just the same, and the trouble is no different. Gil is still sailing *Trilby* somewhere in the Channel, with his conscience —and Sam did not doubt that Gil had a conscience—and Albert is still in hospital, and I am no nearer what to do.' He mooched back to the fire, and watched his mother making pies.

' Is Gil coming home too? ' she asked. ' Where've you left the barge? Is she in the river? '

' She's in Ipswich.' He realized that, having rashly told Agnes about being shelled, it was no good hiding the story from his mother. He did not tell her about Albert though.

'I don't know.' She shook her head darkly. 'Seems it's as bad, wherever you are. You're no better off than Manny. They even got the bombs in Ipswich a few weeks back. Did you hear about that?'

Sam nodded.

'George Young was there. He told us all about it.'

'Pity one didn't drop on him,' Sam said.

'Aye, he's a cocky one these days. Making a mint of money.'

'He ought to join up,' said Sam.

'I don't know. The money though—it doesn't seem right, when Manny gave up a good job to soldier for a shilling a day, and young George was just a butcher's boy. Still, Manny's only himself to blame. I tried hard enough to talk him out of it.'

'You did? But Manny was right! You can't compare Manny and George, can you? Manny's worth ten of George!'

'Manny's a good boy. I only hope to God the war's over before it takes you and Gil.'

'Gil—' Sam shrugged disparagingly. 'He could've gone months ago.'

'He's got more sense.'

Sam didn't want to talk about Gil. His mother's attitude shocked him.

'The women are supposed to want their men to go,' he reminded her indignantly. 'Not talk them out of it! There's posters and things—'

'Yes, and songs—I know! "We don't want to lose you, but we think you ought to go," ' his mother quoted bitterly. 'Some silly girls went and sung that outside little Billy Armstrong's house, and the next day he signed on, and a month later he was dead. You go and ask his mother what she thinks about it!'

Sam shrugged again. His mother was as bad as Bunyard. He sat in the chair by the fire and dozed off. He kept waking up, because it was so quiet, and then dozing and dreaming of Albert. And through all his dozing and waking, he kept wishing desperately that he could join up, but now he was afraid that he wanted to join up for more devious reasons than before: to atone for Gil, and turn his back on the responsibilities he now shouldered. He could not understand why his mother was not ashamed of Gil, as he was, nor why she hesitated to condemn George Young. 'If only Manny would come home,' he kept thinking. 'He would know what to do.' He wondered where Manny was, how far away from Calais. He looked at Manny's letters and saw the heading Bethune, but he did not know where it was.

His mother went out, and when he heard the click of the door latch again, Sam thought it was his mother coming back. He opened his eyes and turned round lazily in the chair, to see Gil standing in the doorway. The shock was not entirely unexpected, but it was an unpleasant awakening.

Gil came in, throwing his cap on the table. Sam felt his insides withdraw, and could not even bring himself to make a conventional greeting. He stayed in the chair, and watched Gil cautiously, dreading to discuss this awful, insoluble thing. Gil looked tired. His face and neck were very brown, from the weather, his eyes wary and restless, not as they had been a year ago. He seemed very much older, not quiet and shy as he had been but, rather, quiet with a watchfulness that—to Sam—spoke of a bad conscience. With everything that lay between them since they last left each other, Sam could not start a conversation. He watched Gil pull out a Woodbine, leaning against the fire-place. His hands were quite steady as he lit it. Sam thought, with a shock of longing, that Gil perhaps had an explanation for all that had happened.

'Is it true that the *Flower* was shelled?' Gil asked. 'That she's in Ipswich for repairs?'

'Yes. The *Notre Dame* shelled her.'

'That's what I heard,' Gil said. 'And Albert, they say, is—' He hesitated.

'He was hit in the head. He's in hospital,' Sam said.

Gil said nothing. Sam looked at him frantically. 'Gil, you—you—' He took a deep breath to steady his tongue. 'What've you done? What were you at Jules's for? Is it true that you—you—' He could not say the word. He could scarcely get the words out. He looked at Gil helplessly, and knew at once that Gil could not comfort him.

'Yes,' Gil said. 'You must know it's true, after that night.'

For all he knew, Sam could not stomach Gil's words. They danced through his brain without meaning. He stared at Gil, eyes like saucers, expecting Gil to dissolve, to scream, to turn into the Devil, to do anything but lean against the fire-place with a Woodbine between his lips. He could find nothing to say, no words to express this violence. Gil's very calm reacted on him: after a minute everything fell into place with dreadful certainty.

'You were giving messages to Jules?'

'Yes.'

Sam leaned his head on his hands, pulling at his rumpled hair. 'But, Gil, you—?' He could not put anything into words. 'Gil—' It was no good. He looked up at Gil again, wondering why Gil was not making excuses, and explanations, but Gil's face was impassive. 'Why?' Sam asked. The word burst out of him. 'Why did you do it?' He looked up at Gil imploringly, begging him to find a reason.

'I did it without knowing what I was doing, and when I found out I—I had to go on,' Gil said, as if it was very simple. 'I can't make any excuses,' he added. And then, 'I don't know what to do.'

'*You* don't know what to do?' Sam repeated.

'It started when Finch burnt his foot,' Gil said. 'When we got to Calais it was pretty bad, and he couldn't walk.

He asked me to take this message to Jules's place. He said it was some money he owed him. When I got back, he said it was worth a lot to him to have got the debt settled, and he gave me some money. He insisted that I take it. He was a bit drunk at the time, as usual, so I didn't argue. I reckoned he owed me some too, for skippering *Trilby* trip after trip, while he boozed. There was a Frog friend of his on board when I got back, and he saw me take the money.' Gil lit another Woodbine from the butt of his old one. 'I didn't think much about it,' he continued, 'until, next trip, Finch wanted me to take another message. I told him to take his own ruddy message, but he said he'd give me twenty pounds if I took it. He said it would make up my pay, for skippering.' Gil paused.

'And you took it?' Sam said.

'Yes.'

Sam groaned. 'You should've—'

'Do you think I don't know what I should have done *now*?' Gil said bitterly. 'I wanted it to spend on—on Agnes,' he added quietly.

Sam groaned again. 'But when you realized—?'

'I didn't want to know. I just went on taking the money. I wanted the money.'

'But—'

'And now I am too deep into it. There are all sorts of things that come into it. Things I can't tell you. And people I can't get away from. They have proof of what I've done. They take great care of things like that. And ways of getting you to do what they want, which aren't nice.'

Gil's voice was flat and cold. Sam could not answer him now, only watch the cigarette smoke curling across the quiet room. There was a fragrance of baking and the dampness of the grass outside. Sam was appalled. His despair of the last few days had at least been tinged with the faint hope that there might be an explanation when Gil turned up, but this desperate honesty of Gil's, crushing dead the merest whisper of any extenuating circumstance, was like being bludgeoned. Sam felt as if he had fallen down a bottomless well.

'What are you going to do?' he whispered.

Gil stubbed out his cigarette. 'I'm going to the "Ferry-Boat" to get drunk,' he said. 'And after that, I don't know.'

When Gil had got enough rum inside him, he called for Agnes Martin. George Young came to the door and told him to clear off, but Gil seized him by the collar of his smart white shirt, pulled him into the road and hit him. Agnes came out, saw George rolling in the dust and laughed. Then Gil told her to get her coat, and they went down the lane, their arms round each other, to where the tide was making silently over the shining mud, and the waders cried along the sea-wall.

8 A Day in the Trenches

Gil came home well after midnight. He slept heavily, but
Sam, lying wakeful in the same room, heard him talking in
his sleep. He said 'Agnes' several times, and then 'Manny,
don't—' and 'don't tell—' and other mumbled, troubled
half-sentences which Sam could not catch. Scruff, lying on
the floor beside the bed, whined when Gil spoke, and thumped
his short tail anxiously. Sam did not fall asleep until the first
yellow streak of dawn was showing over the saltings. When
he awoke later, Gil was lying in bed smoking, one arm
doubled under his head. The sunlight poured into the little
room, and the air outside trembled with the skylarks that
soared over the saltings. Sam sat up, and scratched his head.

' When are you going back? ' he asked.

' This morning,' Gil said. ' We're loading ammunition at Woolwich.'

' You starting on ammunition then? For Calais? '

' Boulogne.'

' Boulogne? You been in there before? '

' Once or twice.'

Sam paused, and scratched his head again. ' What am I supposed to do? ' he asked. ' About all this I know? '

' You do what you like,' Gil said flatly. ' Nobody can tell you.'

' Why—why don't you just push off and enlist? '

Gil did not answer.

' I can't understand you,' Sam said bitterly. ' With Manny and all.'

Gil got up and dressed. He stood at the window, looking out across the river, his face tight and expressionless, saying nothing. Then, with a curt word to Scruff, he went out and down the stairs. Sam heard him saying good-bye to their mother, then the door slammed and the house was quiet.

Sam lay back in bed again. Nothing was solved; everything was as bad—worse—than he had ever envisaged. ' Oh, God,' he thought, ' why did I have to find out? ' If Gil had sworn at him, or lied, or bluffed, it would have made it easier to hate him. But he was the same old Gil he had always got on with all right. In a tight corner he just got quieter, as he had always done. ' But nothing excuses him,' Sam thought. ' He can't just apologize for it. And he didn't even say he was going to pack it in.' He had hinted that he was afraid to pack it in. And afraid of enlisting. ' Afraid,' Sam thought. But was he such a coward? Sam saw him again, as he had seen him bringing *Trilby* into Calais out of a hard Channel wind. It wasn't a completely gutless thing, to sail a barge, week in, week out, through whatever seas God sent; it wasn't a coward's job. 'I can't understand him,' Sam thought hopelessly.

He rolled over in bed, curled up in misery, his hands up to his face. Whatever Gil's motives, it made no difference to Sam's problem: what was *he* to do about it? 'What he's doing,' Sam thought, 'is killing people like Manny.'

'Oh, Manny!' he said out loud. He was the only person in the world Sam knew who could help.

Sam lay very still. The idea took root, slowly, and then with a growing conviction. He jumped out of bed and ran downstairs.

'Good heavens! Aren't you dressing today?' his mother said.

'Those letters of Manny's—where are they?' Sam was peering behind the vase on the chimney shelf. 'I want to know something.'

He found what he wanted and looked at the headings again. The only place-name he could find was the one he had noticed the night before: Bethune. He knew that Manny was in the front line, and the guns that dully thumped in their ears most of the time they were in Calais were the guns of the front line. Surely they could not be much more than fifty miles away? If he were to tell Bunyard that he must see Manny—for some domestic reason he could easily fabricate —he would be able to visit Bethune in the time it took to unload the *Flower*, and be back for her sailing. There was a constant stream of traffic flowing out of Calais for the front, and he did not see that he would have any difficulty in cadging a lift. And somewhere, whatever he was doing, Manny could spare him half-an-hour, if he knew how vital it was, and even if he wasn't able to supply an answer, at least the fact that he knew would lift the suffocating responsibility that Sam found unbearable.

'I must tell someone,' Sam thought desperately. 'It must work.'

The next few days were the longest Sam could ever remember. He went back to the *Flower of Ipswich* and mooched about the yard while the shipwrights sawed and hammered and the riggers put in the new mizzen. At night he slept in his own bunk, amongst the wood shavings that had drifted down the hatch. He felt at home there, far more so than in the cottage at Fambridge, and he had almost a thirst for its dark, safe familiarity, where he could go to ground and not talk to anyone. One of the workmen asked him if he had no home and, rather than explain, Sam said he hadn't, and was much embarrassed the next day by the present of a meat pie. Everyone was talking about the Zeppelin raids, but Sam was merely glad that these comfortable profiteers were getting a dose of war too. ' Do 'em good,' he thought. Nothing pleased him. He was as miserable and restless as a caged bear.

At last the *Flower of Ipswich* had a new deck, and a new mizzen-mast, and new sails, and Bunyard came up from London on the train. As usual, he lost no time. On the next ebb the *Flower* was sailing down the Orwell with Sam on the wheel, past the green woods of Pin Mill where the cuckoos were calling and the smell of warm pine needles came with the breeze. Sam, in a ferment of anxiety, did not notice the serenity of this inland shore slipping past. It was the Calais smell that he was impatient for. The tarry slither of coke was his business, and the Channel his road. This effete yachting irritated him.

' How's Albert? ' had been his first question to Bunyard.

' The Guv'nor had a note from his mother. Said he was getting better.'

The relief Sam felt showed in his face. Bunyard laughed and said, ' Might have knocked some sense into his silly head, with luck ! '

Sam was too nervous to inquire about what had happened to the *Notre Dame de Calais*, but Bunyard told him that she had been impounded by the navy, pending an explanation from her skipper, who had disappeared.

'I reckon he'll stay disappeared, too, if he knows where he's well off,' Bunyard growled. His faded eyes looked very directly into Sam's. Sam could not meet them and looked at Bunyard's white moustache unhappily. 'Don't you?' Bunyard asked.

Sam nodded.

'Where did you get to that night?' Bunyard asked.

'Nowhere.'

'Meddling,' Bunyard said.

Sam was silent.

'I told you not to meddle. You'll learn.'

Sam shook his head. He dared not speak, but Bunyard pressed him no more. 'How much does he know?' Sam wondered miserably. He felt as if his whole secret were written across his face.

The *Flower of Ipswich* carried the flood down the Wallet and into the Swin and was off Southend when the tide turned. It was going dusk, the wind had fallen light, and as Sam laid out the anchor the clanks of the chain links echoed under the pier. A train whistled somewhere. The pier was deserted, and the town lay blinking in the last light of the sun, very quiet for June. Sam stood for a moment, leaning on the forestay, and thought, 'The quiet is because of the war.' He could smell the bacon Bunyard was cooking; a dog barked on the shore and the jellyfish opened and closed like pink flowers as they went down on the tide. Over Kent the first searchlights were scooping the sky. 'It's a Zeppelin night,' Sam thought.

Bunyard had cooked for the two of them, and as they sat together eating, Sam said, 'Is Albert joining us at Beckton, or have we got to find somebody else?'

'Woolwich,' Bunyard said.

'Woolwich? You mean—'

' We're loading munitions this trip.'

Sam was impressed. Munitions were real work, he thought, and he was comforted. He washed up and went to his bunk in the forepeak, but soon after he had got beneath his blanket he heard a distant droning which he could not place. He got up and put his head out of the hatch. The night was cloudless, the sky rashed with stars; but putting them to shame, the Kentish searchlights were making frenzied sweeps round the sky, nervously prodding and stabbing and groping as if they suspected the whole heaven of some secret connivance. It was warm and strange. Sam watched the searchlights' nervous dance until over Sheerness something gleamed momentarily in the sky, diamond-bright. A searchlight overshot, then returned with others, converging hungrily, all weaving one with the other until the bright star shone again, suspended in the web of lights like a fly. To Sam the Zeppelin looked vulnerable and lonely. The guns thumped wildly but the Zeppelin droned on. 'The idiots! The idiots!' Sam said into the darkness. He could hear whistles shrilling on the shore, prompted by the thudding of the guns, but the airship was already away over the marshes on its way to London, following the thread of the narrowing river, and the searchlights could merely point the way of her escape, chastened and then, one by one, extinguished. Disappointed, Sam went back to bed.

The *Flower of Ipswich* was not the only barge loading at Woolwich. Sam looked anxiously along the buoys for *Trilby*, but she was already gone. The *Flower* went alongside and by the time she had settled to her marks with a hundred and fifty tons of shells on board, Albert had once more appeared, as he had appeared the first time Sam had met him at Beckton, waving on the wharf with his kit-bag on his shoulder. He took off his cap and showed Sam his scar, and Sam was duly awed by the new parting in the glossy-black hair and secretly a little jealous. Albert was now a hero.

He told Sam he had spent a marvellous week at home with everyone bringing him presents and the girls all hanging round the door to ask how he was. ' As good as if I'd got it in the trenches,' he said.

Sam thought crossly, ' It could just as easily've been me.' No one had thought him a hero.

At high water the *Flower* got under way, bound for Boulogne. Nervously, Sam watched Bunyard, waiting for an opportunity to put his request. Boulogne was farther from the front than Calais, but there would be plenty of traffic moving out, and Sam was set on seeing Manny. ' If he says no, I'll go anyway,' he thought. Albert was sent below to do some cooking, and Sam was left with Bunyard who was easing the barge past some moored colliers off Tilbury, cursing the fluky wind. Sam waited till he was in the clear, then he cleared his throat and said, ' Mr. Bunyard.'

Bunyard looked at him inquiringly.

' When we get to France, can I—' Sam paused, then forced the words out, ' Can I go and see my brother in the front line, to ask him something? '

' God in heaven! ' said Bunyard.

' I've got to ask him something. It's terribly important— a—domestic thing. I could be there and back in a couple of days. Please, sir, I must.'

Bunyard looked at him. He pushed his cap back and scratched his white head. Sam was screwed up with anxiety, his slate-blue eyes fixed stonily on Bunyard.

' What's wrong? ' Bunyard asked. ' You in trouble? '

Sam did not answer the question. ' It's just something I've got to ask him.'

' If you take my advice, you'd ask someone a bit handier.'

' It's a—a family thing. Only Manny will do.'

Bunyard shrugged. ' You go then. You'll get your silly head blown off, as like as not.' He looked at Sam with an exasperated, yet not unaffectionate, expression. Fortunately for Sam, an overtaking steamer then took Bunyard's attention, and by the time he had finished a bawling match with the skipper on the bridge, the request was forgotten. Sam nursed Bunyard's brief reply: ' You go then.' He was not bothered about the qualification. He even began to feel excited about the prospect—an excitement that had nothing to do with the purpose of his mission, but purely with the fact that he was going to see the front line. Or at least, as near as he could get. In a tangle of mixed fear and excitement, he nearly gybed the *Flower* going down Sea Reach, and Bunyard swore at him furiously.

When Albert found out about Sam's intentions, he was astonished.

' Why, you can't just walk in the trenches and say, " Where's me brother? " There's blokes standing around saying, " Halt, who goes there? " and shooting people like you.'

' I can get a message to him,' Sam said. ' And he can get to see me.'

' What's it all about, anyway? ' Albert asked. ' Why can't you write him a letter? '

' It's something private,' Sam said stubbornly.

' You're barmy,' Albert said. He was peeling potatoes on the foredeck, and Sam was whipping a new heaving line.

' That night you followed Gil,' Albert said, ' was it anything to do with Jules lobbing those shells at us? '

Sam studied his work with care. The question did not surprise him, but, with all the forewarning in the world, there was no answer.

' How should I know? ' he said.

' Very well, I should think,' Albert said.

' Well, I'm not saying.'

' Did Gil go there? '

Sam did not answer. If he said no, he knew that Albert would know he was lying. Perhaps Bunyard knew why

Jules shelled them too. Perhaps, even, they both knew what he wanted to ask Manny. But Sam could not bring himself to speak about it, even with Albert. A tacit silence was all he asked and, to his relief, Albert granted it, peeling his potatoes with unusual care, so that spirals of potato-peeling revolved steadily into the bucket.

'Tide's slack,' Sam said.

'Well, he's not stopping,' Albert said, glancing aft at their skipper.

'Not with this wind,' Sam agreed.

The *Flower of Ipswich* butted round the North Forland in a freshening westerly. The night was very short, the stars paling before four o'clock over the downs above Cap Gris Nez. Sam watched the coast slip past, the dun sands and the huddled village beneath the shadow of the downs, and he felt the excitement rising in him at the thought of the day ahead. The *Flower* crashed along, swilling her decks, towards the long harbour wall of Boulogne. A hospital ship was coming out, her decks crowded with men in khaki, and on her heels a barge was setting her jib, ducking into the swell off the harbour mouth.

'It's *Trilby*,' Albert said.

Gil, at the wheel, lifted a hand in greeting. Bunyard and Albert waved, but Sam stood with his hands in his pockets. The *Flower* heeled past, close under the lighthouse, and Sam looked across the wide outer harbour towards the shore, where the cranes made familiar patterns against the crawling hill of roofs and walls beyond. In half-an-hour he could be on his way. The sight of *Trilby* strengthened his determination. The shock he had experienced at seeing her, the repulsion like a sickness in his stomach, hardened into this tingling excitement again. 'Whatever Manny says,' he thought, 'I will do. He will know.' The desire to see Manny now was the only thought in his head, almost shutting out the reason. Sam kept picturing Manny's wiry figure, his

quiet, certain way, the dark-red moustache against the brown skin. Sam had never seen him in khaki, and his picture blurred. He could only see him in a cap and a bargeman's jersey, faded with the weather.

It took an hour to find *Flower* a berth and make her fast, alongside a coaster full of gas cylinders. As soon as all was in order, Sam asked Bunyard for permission to go.

'Aye, but I'm not waiting if you're not back, remember,' the skipper said. 'And watch what you're doing, you silly young devil.'

'Yes, sir.'

He climbed up to the quay and hurried away before anything happened to stop him. He had plenty of money on him and some cigarettes but nothing else. The money was tied up in a handkerchief and knotted round his waist

with a bit of lashing for safe keeping, and the cigarettes he had bundled in his jersey under his arm. He knew that he was heading for Bethune, which he believed was about fifty miles away, but beyond that he knew nothing.

Boulogne harbour was very much bigger than Calais. Sam was sweating before he had even crossed the bridge into the town. He thought if he walked out of the town on to the road running east, he would get a lift in a lorry or wagon, but as he hurried up the main street he began to hope fervently that this modest desire would be granted, for walking fifty miles in the hot sun after a night at sea was not an attractive thought. The cobbled streets were crowded, climbing steeply away from the sea to where the dome of a cathedral glinted against a hazy blue sky. A street market spilled colour and noise against the steps of an old church, but Sam did not stop to inspect it. He pushed through the milling women in their black peasant's skirts with their baskets of vegetables and chickens tied by the legs, and the same feeling of repulsion came to him that he had experienced at home. ' They're doing all right out of the war,' he thought. The port had never been busier. Faintly, like distant thunder, the gunfire shivered the sky, but nobody took any notice. Sam had his face towards it like a pilgrim, hurrying up the hill, despising the avaricious French as he went, eager— almost thirsty—to be where the guns were firing. ' If only I were old enough! ' he thought. ' I could be going there properly.' This eagerness propelled him up over the hot cobbles to where the road bore round under the ramparts of the old town. The sea sparkled below; the bells of the cathedral spun lazily over the town, drowning the gunfire, and Sam took the road for St. Omer, stubbornly keeping up his pace.

In a quarter of an hour he got a lift in a horse-drawn fish-cart. It was not fast, but it was better than walking, and Sam, curled up on the bottom boards, lulled by the clip of the horse's hooves, stopped worrying for the first time for days. Half-asleep, heading in the right direction, he became aware of a sense of freedom that was completely new to him. He realized that he was doing exactly what he wanted, answerable to no one, and that there was no reason at all why he should be back in Boulogne when the *Flower* sailed, if he chose otherwise. He had plenty of money. Even the reason for his journey slipped to the back of his mind, and he lay savouring this strange lightness of the spirit until, abruptly, the fish-cart arrived at its destination and he had to climb down.

His next lift was in a motor-lorry with two Frenchmen. Sam got in the back, which was empty, and slept heavily, undisturbed by the jolting of the hard tyres. When he awoke the lorry had stopped, and when he climbed up and looked out he saw that it was parked outside a café in a village street. The street was dusty and empty. Beyond the low, white-washed houses were marshy fields fringed with willow and poplars. A meandering stream, tangled with yellow water-flags, crossed under the street a little farther on; Sam could see some children splashing about by the bridge and hear the cool murmur of the water. Covered with dust and sweat, Sam watched the peaceful landscape with a strange longing. Awakened to it, suddenly, and without warning, it seemed like something out of a story-book. The cows, mildly browsing in the green pastures, were of a nursery-rhyme timelessness, the wild red poppies crushed beneath their feet. Far more real to Sam, and yet disregarded by the few people in their doorways and the shouting children, was the thudding and rumbling in the sky. The interlude remained vividly stamped in Sam's mind long after the lorry had continued its bumpy journey: he could not reconcile the placid village and the playing children with the trembling sky.

In the late afternoon the lorry dropped him at a crossroads. The driver pointed down one of the arms and said, ' Bethune. *Quinze kilometres.*' He held up the five fingers of one hand three times, and pointed again. The other man said, ' Bethune . . . attention ! ' and did a mime of a shell coming over and a big explosion. Then they both laughed, shook his hand, wished him *bon voyage* and drove away down the side road. Sam started walking. He supposed that ' *quinze* ' was fifteen, and thought that kilometres must be much like miles. ' I can be there tonight,' he thought, ' even walking.'

Most of the traffic that passed him now was military. A Staff Officer's tourer roared past in a cloud of dust. Coming the other way, a long line of pack-horses hurried for home in the charge of two corporals, the thick golden light of the evening sun glossing the sweat on their necks. Sam walked on, fast, excited, past the occasional brick farm-houses with their chickens going to roost and the cow fields smelling of damp grass. Another long line of transport horses passed him, harnessed to limbers, then a straggling of troops, very dirty and weary. Sam, used to gleaming boots and buttons and crisply moving arms, was puzzled, and thought perhaps the men were French. He stared at them as they went past, at the ragged khaki and the tired, unshaven faces, and was surprised to find that he could understand the muttered—and mostly blasphemous—remarks that were being bandied amongst them: the men were Welsh.

As dusk came, with faint lines of damp mist rising from the fields, Sam came to the outskirts of Bethune. An old grey town with busy cafés, dimmed lights and cobbled streets echoing to the rumble of passing carts, Bethune quivered to the guns beyond. The barrage had sharpened from the dull thudding above the St. Omer hills to a sharp noisy succession of explosions near at hand; occasionally Sam saw flashes in the sky, or the pale arc of a flare outlining the roofs. But in the town, as in the country village earlier, no one was concerned. Two little girls in pinafores scurried by on an errand, giggling at Sam. He followed them slowly down the street, not a bit tired any more but quivering with a nervous excitement that made him feel almost light-headed. Two soldiers were standing on a corner. Sam went up to them.

' Please, I'm looking for my brother—'

' Who's he? General Haig?'

' If it was your sister, now—' the other one said.

They stood grinning.

' He's in the Royal Engineers,' Sam said.

' Lot o' blokes in the R.E.s,' said the soldier.

' At Cambrin.'

' Straight on,' said the other soldier, pointing up the street. ' Can't miss it.'

' Where all the bangs are,' the other one said.

' How far? '

' It's about six, seven miles.'

They looked at him curiously. Their uniforms were

filthy, their faces lined and stubbled. 'What are you doin'? Just visiting?'

'Just dropping in for a cup of tea and a chat?' the other one inquired.

'Sort of,' Sam said awkwardly.

'I hope he's expecting you,' the soldier said, very grave. 'So's he can get the clean cloth out, and the best china.'

The two of them roared with laughter. Sam walked on, feeling uncomfortable. Nothing was quite like he had expected, now. He felt uncertain, somehow having visualized himself reporting to some orderly barracks and meeting Manny in a polished room. He hurried on, through the cobbled main square where the clock on the massive stone tower pointed to ten o'clock, and out past the struggling houses into a darkness lit only by gun flashes ahead. Nervous excitement drove him, so that he did not count the miles he had walked. He was mesmerized by the lights in the sky, and the noise, and was frightened in a strange, almost enjoyable way. He tried to think what it would be like if he were a soldier, going to the front line whether he liked it or not. 'But now I can run away, if I want,' he thought, and it was this fact that comforted him, and kept him going on.

As he approached the line of the British batteries, the noise was deafening. The guns were off the road, out of sight in the darkness, but when he had passed them the salvoes of whining shells came from behind, hissing over his head. The first time he dived into the grass, panic-stricken. His mouth was full of dust, his hands sticky with sweat and his heart thumped hard against the crushed cigarettes he still carried. He realized suddenly that he was crazy, to be looking for Manny in such a place, but as he grovelled there a column of soldiers marched past him, going in the same direction, and when another salvo came over and he had ducked again, he realized that the soldiers were still marching, and the tune they were singing had not even wavered. He could hear the

ragged thudding of their boots receding up the road and, rather ashamed, he stood up, straightened his cap, and walked on. But his first enthusiasm for Cambrin was waning.

He noticed the shell-holes gaping in the roof of an empty cottage beside the road; he could look up through its rafters into the starry sky. He remembered the night before, looking up at the same stars from the deck of the *Flower of Ipswich*, and his journey to Cambrin seemed to have lasted for days, so long ago did it seem. He stood there for a bit, and the guns were silent. The soldiers had disappeared into the darkness. A bunch of ragwort thrust up through the doorstep of the cottage under his feet and shone gold against the darkness of his trousers.

'Perhaps Manny isn't up here anyway,' he thought.

He was hungry and very thirsty. He went round to the back of the cottage and found a pump, and after a lot of creaking and clanking on the handle he was rewarded with a stream of icy water. He drank some and ran it over his dirty, sticky face. While he was still bending over it he heard a screaming, crescendoing whine over his head, and he dropped flat, his arms over his head. The earth rocked beneath him, and a red flash lit his vision. The pump-handle rattled in the blast, and some slates shivered and dropped off the roof of the cottage with a clatter on to the stones. Sam lifted his head gingerly. There was a smell of cordite, and a refreshing odour of damp earth, thrown up by the shell. Sam knew that this particular explosion was from a German gun, aimed from the direction he was walking in, and he thought he was being stupid to go on. He stood hesitantly.

'But I've come so far,' he thought crossly.

He did not know what to do.

'You've only got to be a bit nearer to one of those,' he told himself.

The British guns had opened up again, and he shivered as the shells came up out of the darkness, with their blood-freezing noise. The ruined cottage trembled and another slate fell. Then, as he hesitated, he heard the sound of voices down the road, coming from Bethune. Four soldiers were coming towards him with a loaded handcart, swearing happily. Sam stepped forward out of the shadow of the cottage, and they stopped short of him. One of them had his rifle at the ready, Sam noticed, and so he spoke quickly:

'I'm looking for my brother. He's in the R.E.s at Cambrin. Goodchild—Manny Goodchild. Do you know him?'

'Cor strike me! That's cool,' one of the men said.

'Can I come with you?'

'What d'you think we are? Conducted tour?'

'I've got some cigarettes . . .' Sam held out a packet, which was accepted with alacrity.

'I'd take you to the Kaiser for a packet of fags. Who d'you want? Goodchild?'

'Never 'eard of 'im,' said another.

'Plenty of R.E.s at Cambrin. You can come up if you like.'

They argued briefly amongst themselves as to the risk they were running in allowing Sam to come with them, but another packet of cigarettes persuaded them, and Sam was allowed to tag along behind. The handcart was full of what appeared to be pit-props, which Sam gathered were for supporting the trenches. The four men were a fatigue party and belonged to a Middlesex regiment. With their support, Sam felt far happier, and was even able to affect a nonchalance when the shells screamed overhead again. He was by now utterly weary, and the night took on a dream-like sensation, in which the scream of the shells was spaced out with strange moonlit intervals of perfect calm, when all the lights in the sky were merely stars, and the smells of the earth the ordinary pungency of wet cow-pasture. The cart rattled on the cobbled road. A row of poplars, some lopped by gunfire, rustled softly in the breeze. Instinctively Sam sniffed the wind, and thought, 'Fair for Dover.'

On the outskirts of Cambrin the fatigue party told him the R.E.s were boring under the German lines. 'He'll be one of that lot, I dare say.' They waved a vague arm eastward towards a dishevelled wood, black against the sky, and left him, pushing their cart stubbornly into the darkness.

Sam was too tired to think what to do. He stumbled across a field towards the trees. Skirting one of the shell-holes which pitted his path he almost fell into a deep ditch. It seemed recently dug, and when he made out telephone wires stapled along one side of it he realized that he was actually in a trench. He walked along it gingerly, thinking to himself, stupidly, 'I'm in the trenches,' but when he did not meet anyone, he began to wonder if he were being very wise. The sky ahead was bright with flares and flashes, and irregular thumps. He tripped over a looped wire, and scarcely had the strength to get to his feet again. The trench gave him a feeling of security, and when a few yards farther on he found a pile of old sacks, he sat down to have a rest. He remembered feeling very hungry, then no more until someone was shaking him, and there was a smell of wood-smoke and bacon frying which came to his returning consciousness with an exquisite sensation of longing.

He found himself opening his eyes to the barrel of a rifle. Beyond it was a squat red face with hostile eyes, saying, 'Strewth! Look what's 'ere!'

Sam struggled into a sitting position, pierced with cramps, and found himself facing two khaki-clad figures. The rifle beckoned him brusquely to get to his feet.

'What's all this then? Where d'you come from? Who are you?' barked the man behind the rifle. The other figure looked on, slightly amused.

'I—I'm looking for my brother. Private Goodchild. Manny Goodchild—' Sam still felt dazed. The air was cold and fresh, the sky misty with dawn. Sam's feet slithered in the wet clay. He could still smell the bacon, and his stomach turned over with desire.

'Goodchild? He's in the tunnel, sir.' The man turned to the officer behind him. 'Copped it last night.'

The officer nodded. 'I know him. They took him down to the Aid Post.' He looked at Sam reflectively. 'There's a marked resemblance,' he pointed out to the N.C.O., who put up his rifle. 'All the same,' he continued to Sam, 'you don't come up here visiting, my lad. It's not home from home.'

'I've got to talk to him, sir. I come over to Calais, regular, on a barge, and I thought I could just see him, just for a minute. To ask him something. It's—it's about something at home—' Sam, suddenly, was desperate in case, having come so far, and at last found someone who knew Manny, he was going to be dispatched back the way he had come, unsatisfied.

'I dare say it can be arranged,' the officer said, quite kindly. 'But you'll have to wait for an escort to go back. You can't just wander around here on your own. You'll get shot.'

'Shall I take him down a dug-out, sir? Till someone's going back?'

'Yes. Do that.'

To Sam's relief, he was led farther along the trench towards the smell of bacon. The officer remained behind, and Sam said to his escort, 'What did you say about my brother? Copped it . . . you mean wounded? What—is he—is he all right, I mean?'

'He's a good 'un, your brother, else I wouldn't take so much trouble with you, young fellow-me-lad,' the N.C.O. said. 'Yes, he copped it last night. A nice cushy one, so you'd 'ave seen 'im at 'ome if you'd 'ad a bit of patience. Get in 'ere now.' He stopped suddenly, and while Sam was still wondering what a 'nice cushy one' was, he found himself pushed down some muddy steps and into a smoky hole full of feet and rifles which he fell over. The N.C.O. shouted something down after him, then turned and disappeared to join the officer.

Sam, his eyes streaming with the smoke, tried to take in

his surroundings. The dug-out appeared to be merely an embrasure in the side of the trench, roofed over with old timber, cramped and sticky. The floor was wet clay. The fire that was making so much smoke was being refuelled by one of the men with what looked like a big biscuit, and the bacon smell was hot and strong. There were two men in the dug-out, who introduced themselves as Taffy and Batty. Along with the introduction Sam got a hunk of hard bread and a piece of bacon. By the time he had explained his mission, he was beginning to see more clearly. The food warmed him, and a tinful of thick, syrupy tea went down like nectar. Outside, skylarks were twittering above the trench. Then a sudden explosive crack, apparently just over his head, made Sam jump and spill his tea.

' What's that? '

The two men had not even blinked. ' Rifle-shot,' said Taffy briefly. ' Makes that noise, when it crosses the trench,' he explained.

' Nothing to worry about, if you keep your head down,' said Batty happily.

The two men were signallers, whose job was to repair the wires that ran up the communication trench to the front line. When they went out of the dug-out, following up their wire, Sam went with them, sweating now as the shells whined across from the German lines, compelling Sam to flinch and duck. Taffy and Batty seemed to disregard them. Taffy even told Sam, 'It's quiet, this morning.' Between whiles Sam could still hear the skylarks. The sun was shining out of a cloudless sky, and the shell-holes were rimmed with blue cornflowers. Big rats scuttered over the sand-bags above his head. Sam was shivering, and his stomach was cold again. Batty suddenly shoved him down, face-first into the mud, and a great crash seemed to lift the ground up beneath him and drop it again. Earth showered down, and bits of shell casing plopped viciously into the red ground.

'Near one,' said Batty equably. He was stubbled and filthy, his khaki almost in rags, but a pair of blue eyes considered Sam sympathetically. 'We've checked the lot when we get to the top. We'll take you back then.'

'It's—not like I expected,' Sam said.

Batty laughed. 'Not like any of us expected, really,' he said easily. 'You get used to it,' he added.

They had to flatten themselves against the side of the trench as an awkward procession of stretcher bearers came past, slipping and grunting and swearing. There were three stretchers. Sam tried not to look, but his eyes were riveted against his will on the three wounded men. They were wrapped in bloody blankets. The last one was crying out, with a dreadful noise that Sam had never heard before, and the man at his head said to him, 'You're all right, mate. It's a nice cushy one you've got. It's Blighty for you.'

'You can go down with them if you like,' Taffy said to Sam. 'They're going down to the Aid Post.'

Sam stayed with his back pressed against the wall. He shook his head. The swearing men had passed and disappeared along the trench, and Taffy and Batty were following their wire again, restapling it where it hung loose. Sam licked his lips.

'What—what's a "cushy one"?' he whispered to Taffy. His voice sounded strange.

'Means you can go home,' Taffy said. 'It's what everyone wants, a nice cushy one.'

Is that what Manny's got? Sam wondered. Something that would make him cry out like the bloody heap on the stretcher? He shivered. Taffy was laughing at something Batty had said.

'Keep your head down,' Batty said to Sam, as another rifle crack echoed down the trench.

Sam found that his knees were trembling. He followed Batty and Taffy, stumbling and crawling and ducking, until at last they told him they were finished. ' We've got to go back for wire,' Batty said. ' We'll take you down, and you can find your brother.' Sam followed them blindly back the way they had come, back past the dug-out and past the sacks where he had slept, through the shambles of a big shell-hole and through the broken trees. It was very hot, but Sam felt cold inside. The Aid Post was a ruined farm-house, and the three stretchers that had passed earlier lay outside. The man who had been crying out was now silent. Sam did not look this time, but asked a medical orderly if he knew anything of Manny.

' He was wounded last night. He's got red hair . . . a red moustache.' He almost added, ' And a cushy one.'

' All the ones we had in last night went down to Bethune,' the orderly said. ' They don't stay here long when it's quiet.'

' Is that where he'll be now?'

' Yes. Unless he's been put on a train. They go on to Boulogne, if they're going home.'

Sam hurried on aghast. Suppose Manny was on his way back to Boulogne, after this long, nightmarish journey? Had they both been in Bethune last night, passing each other by? Sam was shattered by his morning's experiences, and kept hearing the awful cries of the man who had got a ' cushy one '. The broken poplars cast a withered shade, and the cobbled road wound on back to Bethune, shimmering in the heat. The shells came over from the British guns, hissing overhead, the great thunder of the explosions shivering the dusty grass beside the road. Sam felt that his head was full of noise, the cries and the explosions, and all through it were Taffy's complacent words, ' It's quiet, this morning.'

The sweat trickled down his face as he limped into Bethune for the second time. The grey-faced houses with their deep shade were comforting after the hazards of the open country-side. Some mess-carts rumbled past, and then, incongruously,

a London bus full of troops. Sam asked a soldier where to
find Manny, and the soldier told him the way to a school
that had been taken over as a casualty clearing station. A
Ford ambulance stood in the yard, being loaded with
stretchers whose loads were ominously still and shrouded.
The two orderlies doing the loading were discussing the
dimensions of a certain Mademoiselle Yvonne with much
ribaldry, and Sam stood shaking, picturing Manny's face
under every blanket. He, who had considered himself so
brave, was shocked at every turn. With a great effort he
pulled himself together and, avoiding the ambulance,
walked up the steps and through the door. 'It's because of
Manny,' he said to himself. 'What's a load of stiffs to me,
except for Manny?' But he could not stop himself shaking.

Inside the school, a French nun stood talking to a man in
khaki. Another nun whisked past carrying a bucket but took
no notice of Sam. Stone stairs led up out of the narrow hall,
scrubbed white, and through open doors Sam could see
beds pushed close together and stretchers with men on them
lined up at the bottom of the beds. The nun and the medical
officer looked at him curiously, but went on talking. He
waited till they had finished, and then the officer said to him,
'What do you want?' and once more he launched into his
description of Manny.

'Last night? Well, if he's here, he'll probably be on one
of the stretchers.' The man did not seem very interested, and
resumed his conversation with the nun, and Sam forced
himself to walk on into the room that opened out of the hall,
where the stretchers filled the whole of the centre of the
floor. Almost immediately he saw Manny. He was lying
near the door, a blanket over him. His eyes were closed, his
face stubbled and dirty. Flies buzzed over a smear of blood
on his forehead, but Manny did not stir.

Sam stepped over two other stretchers to get to him, and
squatted down beside him.

'Manny!' he whispered desperately. 'Manny! It's me, Sam.'

His voice shook. For a moment he thought Manny was one of the cases destined for the ambulance outside the door, and he hit the flies away in an agony of fear. Manny's eyes opened, and focused with difficulty on Sam. It seemed an age to Sam before any emotion stirred in them. They stared at him, the familiar slate-blue eyes that could just as well have been Gil's, but they said nothing.

'Manny!' Sam squeaked. 'It's Sam! Don't you know me?'

'Sam!' Manny's lips moved silently, and his eyes recognized Sam. They travelled over his face, slowly, with a dawning pain and bewilderment.

'Sam,' he said again, silently.

'Oh, Manny! Are you all right? Please—' Sam tried to pull himself together. It was not for Manny to help him, he realized with a great stab of light, but for him to help Manny. The inane shaking stopped, and he suddenly felt very calm and, for the first time in what felt days, sure of himself.

'You're all right,' he said. 'A nice cushy one.'

Manny smiled faintly.

'You'll be going home,' Sam said softly. 'You'll be all right.'

Manny's face was grey, and the red hair stood out vividly in contrast. Sam had never seen him looking like this before. He found his eyes straying to the blanket that covered him, for some indication of how he was wounded, but it revealed nothing, and he dared not ask. Besides, Manny could not speak. A bead of sweat trickled down the side of his nose. Sam wiped it away.

'We're doing the Channel trip, once—twice—a week,' he said. 'So I thought I'd look you up. I'm still on the *Flower*.' He talked at random, terrified of Manny's silence. Some

orderlies were taking some of the stretchers away, the nun
pointing out which men to take. But when they indicated
Manny she shook her head.

' *Trop malade.*'

Sam did not know that it meant ' Too ill.' Manny's eyes
were shut again, and Sam got up and went over to the nun.

' Will he be all right? ' he asked. ' The one with red hair.'

The nun turned and said something, swiftly and in-
comprehensibly, but with a quick, sympathetic smile. The
Medical Officer came in and said to the orderlies, ' That's
the lot for the station then? '

' Yes, sir.'

The orderlies went out and the officer went to follow
them, but Sam caught him by the arm. ' Please, sir—'

' What is it? '

' Will he be all right, my brother? ' He pointed to Manny,
who was lying as Sam had first seen him, with his eyes shut.
He now felt, with even more urgency
than he had felt for his original problem,
that the answer to this question was what
he had made this journey for. The officer
was not impatient. He looked at Manny,
and stroked his chin thoughtfully.

' He's got a bad one, in the stomach. With luck, he'll survive.'

Sam looked at the officer bleakly.

' With luck?'

' If he's tough enough, and with a bit of luck, yes,' said the officer.

There was nothing else to ask, or do. Sam went back to Manny and stood looking down on him. He said, ' I've got to go back to the *Flower* now, Manny.' But Manny neither saw nor heard him.

9 Zeppelin

Sam got back to Boulogne late the same night, and found the *Flower* still in her berth. She was unloaded, and Bunyard was on deck, so Sam had no chance to avoid him.

' So you're still in the land of the living? '

' Yes.'

' You saw him? '

Sam nodded.

' Everything all right now? '

Bunyard's gruff voice was not impatient, or angry. Sam could make out his features in the flare of the arc lights that lit the quays at night, and he knew that Bunyard was aware that something was wrong. He half-guessed, too, that Bunyard knew what it was.

' He's been wounded,' Sam said. A wave of self-pity overtook him. He was almost asleep on his feet, with nothing accomplished for his journey, save the doubling of his anxieties.

' That's bad,' Bunyard said.

Manny's grey face reeled through Sam's head. He could see nothing else. And Gil *helping*. . . . He gave a sort of snort, almost a sob, and leaned against the shrouds.

' Drop of rum'd suit you just now,' Bunyard said. He jerked his head towards the after-hatch, and Sam went gratefully down into the hot, poky little cabin, where Bunyard poured him out a glass of rum.

' Brainless little puppy,' Bunyard was growling. ' Get into the bunk. Sleep it off.'

It was his rough sympathy that finished Sam, dissolved all his thoughts into one miasma of despair, nothing any longer delineated. He buried himself in Bunyard's bunk, unresisting, and slept.

The *Flower of Ipswich* left Boulogne and was half-way to Dover before Sam was woken by Albert cooking breakfast on the fire. Albert, never the most delicate of workers, had dropped an iron frying-pan with a resounding clang and a string of bad language close beside Sam's ear. Sam woke to the familiar roll and creak of the working barge, and remembered everything instantly. He watched Albert break eight eggs into the frying-pan and stir them with a vigorous fork, and sat up guiltily.

'Didn't the old man call me, then?'

'Ruddy favouritism,' Albert said. He shook the pan energetically. It was hot in the cabin and his face shone over the fire. He pushed his cap back, his eyes concentrating on the eggs. 'You see Manny, then?'

'Yes,' Sam said.

'Bunyard said he's wounded.'

'Yes. He was bad.' Sam thought, 'He might be dead by now.' He sat up on the edge of the bunk and watched Albert absently.

'Queer, you going just when he got wounded,' Albert said.

'Yes.'

Albert stirred the eggs again, rather impatiently. After a few seconds' silence he said, 'Right chatterbox you are.'

'Oh, lay off!' Sam said angrily. He did not want to talk about it. He got out of the bunk, pulled his boots on and went up on deck. Bunyard gave him the wheel, and went down for his breakfast, and Sam was alone. He realized, as he stood there, that he did not enjoy his own company any more than Albert's. 'Manny could've been doing this now, if he'd chosen,' he thought, as the barge turned up an easy wake across a glittering Channel. 'Just like a holiday.' He eased the wheel, checking her course, and thought, 'This time yesterday I was in the trenches.' He dared not think any further.

Bunyard came up, wiping his moustache, and stood beside him. Sam concentrated on his job, but Bunyard merely said, ' Better go and get fed while it's hot. Then you can take her.'

Sam went back below and Albert pushed a plateful of eggs towards him. He said nothing, on his dignity, but Sam, morosely picking at the eggs, said, ' I don't know what to do.' He could not keep it to himself any longer.

Albert's eyes gleamed. He leaned across the table. ' About Gil, you mean? That's why you went to see Manny?'

' Yes. And Manny was wounded and I couldn't tell him, so now I don't know what to do.'

' Gil went to Jules?'

Sam nodded, unable to look at Albert.

' And you've spoken to Gil since? You must have. What did he say?'

Sam told Albert of the painful conversation he had had with Gil. ' He didn't tell me I mustn't give him away. He just said, " Do what you like." He's—he's not doing it because—because—' Sam stabbed blindly at his eggs. He could not think of the words.

' Because he's a Hun-lover?'

' He's not a real spy,' Sam said helplessly. ' Just sort of—of mixed up in it.'

' It's Finch?' Albert said.

' Yes, but Gil should have told on Finch, not helped him,' Sam said. ' Now, he says he can't stop. As if he's frightened.'

' Yes, because he knows he's done enough to get him-self into trouble. If he splits on Finch, Finch'll split on him.'

' But if we know, and don't say anything, it's just as bad,' Sam said. ' And seeing it yesterday, and Manny like that, all those blokes—that bloke on the stretcher screaming out—

and them all working and sweating up there, and getting killed—and Gil—Gil *helping*—'

Sam pushed the eggs away. 'God Almighty!' he said. 'If he'd seen it! And that Taffy, he said it was a quiet day. "It's quiet, this morning," he said. And those ruddy stretchers all laid out in rows.'

He looked at Albert, appalled, the sweat breaking out on his forehead.

'I can't not do anything!'

Albert looked shaken.

'You'll tell on him, then? To the police?'

But Sam could not visualize it. He shook his head. 'Perhaps Mr. Bunyard . . .'

'You could tell him now.'

'No, not now!'

'Before Gil makes another trip,' Albert said. 'If you're going to at all, it's no good waiting.'

'Yes. And perhaps if I see him in Woolwich—if I tell him about Manny—if I see him again, I might stop him. Make him go away somewhere.' Sam was clutching at straws.

'If we make a fast passage, we might see him,' Albert agreed.

'I must!' Sam said. Pressed now to face facts, he could not see himself telling Bunyard without making one last effort to deflect Gil from his course. If he told Gil about Manny. . . .

'I must see Gil! Then, if not . . . I'll tell Bunyard.'

A decision of some sort was better than no decision at all. Sam could see an end to his dilemma. Surely, if Gil knew about Manny, he would come to his senses?

The *Flower of Ipswich* made a fast, easy passage, but not fast enough for Sam. He stared grimly at the long bowsprit raking forward, dipping and lifting with a complaining of tried timber as the Channel miles slipped astern. He gnawed uncertainly at his thumb-nails, restlessly moving from one job to another. Albert said no more, and Bunyard watched Sam, and said nothing. Their passage up the Thames was delayed by the naval patrol. They were forced to miss a fair tide; even Bunyard's swearing did not move the patrol officer, and Sam stood by bleakly as the chain ran out, and the moon came up over the great, calm estuary. Nothing moved on the water, save a hovering gull over the sand. The searchlights played their nervous game, and Sam could not sleep, watching them through the open hatch, and thinking of Manny. Was Manny's luck holding? he wondered.

Trilby'll be loaded by now,' Albert said. ' I bet we pass her coming down.'

The *Flower of Ipswich* was allowed to move at dawn and Sam felt that both Bunyard and Albert shared his relief equally. Did Bunyard know? Sam guessed that his anxiety was showing, and he knew that Bunyard missed little, standing massively at the wheel, watching the river with his faded eyes, gentling the big barge on her awkward winding course. Gravesend . . . Tilbury . . . ' We'll just make it on the flood,' Albert said.

' With luck.'

The summer sky was hazy with the old London grime; the water flowed thick and sluggish. Sam was thinking of Manny and the sweat on his face, and the fly on the smear of blood. Topmasts showed ahead. Beckton Gasworks belched forth its plumes of sulphurous flame, Barking creek brimmed between the rubbish-strewn marshes and the gulls squawked among the sewage. When the ebb started, the barges at Woolwich would start coming down, Sam thought—if they had not already gone. A kind zephyr pressed the *Flower* into Woolwich reach; Sam peered frantically amongst the traffic, but Bunyard was shouting at him to start brailing up the mainsail. Albert had the warps ready, and was dropping the anchor down below the stem, to prevent damage when going alongside. The tide was slack. The *Flower* inched towards the tier where two empty barges lay and, at a nod from Bunyard, Sam started winding up the mains. The folds of canvas gathered themselves up, stiff but easy, withdrawing to reveal to Sam the squat shape of the Woolwich Arsenal. The *Flower*, held by her topsail, hung on the turning tide. A boy stood on the foredeck of the moored barge ahead, waiting to take the warp that Albert was getting ready to heave across. Everything was in order, calm and well-judged (as usual, with Bunyard) and Sam had time to look round before winching in the middle and lower brails. Almost immediately he saw *Trilby*. She was lying alongside the wharf, half-loaded, and Gil was sitting on the hatch coaming with Scotty, eating. It was the dinner break, Sam realized, with a shock at anything so completely normal. ' But it won't be normal,' he thought, ' not when I get across to him.' Bunyard gave him a nod and he brailed the mainsail right up to the throat, and let go the topsail halyards. Albert had made fast up forward to the empty barge already moored. He was lowering the rowing-boat now, to take warps out to the buoys. Sam fed the warps out, impatient to get through this tedious drill, get the barge moored up and tidy, so that he could go across to *Trilby*. ' At least,' he thought with satisfaction, ' she won't be catching this tide.' She was barely half-way down to her marks.

When their jobs were finished, he sculled across to *Trilby*. Although he had his back to her, he could feel Gil watching him, eating his bread and cold sausage, and drinking beer from a mug. He heard Scotty shout, ' Old Bunyard let you have time off for visiting? He must be getting soft.'

Sam dug in his blade and put the boat alongside where Gil and Scotty were sitting, and reached up and held the shipped leeboard. Gil got up and looked down on him, leaning on the shrouds.

' What d'you want? '

' I came to tell you I went to see Manny last trip,' Sam said.

Gil's expression changed. He was startled, and the hard look went out of his face.

'What did you do that for?'

'I wanted his advice,' Sam said.

'What did he say?' Gil spoke quickly, the colour coming up into his face, his eyes full of shame. 'You told him—about—?'

'I was going to, but he's been wounded. He was very bad, he couldn't say anything at all. He couldn't speak. The doctor said he might live, with luck.'

Sam did not intend to spare Gil. He saw Gil's face seem to sag, the lips quiver, the eyes widen with shock. For a moment Sam was filled with compassion, and with the old affection he had always had for Gil.

'You must stop, Gil,' he said urgently, aware of Scotty listening. 'With—with Manny and all—' He could not put such a confusion of torn loyalties into words. He hung on the leeboard, feeling the tide running beneath his feet, trying to pluck the rowing-boat away. He fixed his eyes on Gil's face, aware that the current between them was as strong as the tide itself: Gil's answer could reconcile, or put them irrevocably apart. Sam's arm ached with holding the rowing-boat.

'If you'd seen him, Gil—'

Gil shrugged. His face was closed up again, the conflict withdrawn into the blue-grey, troubled eyes. He shook his head. 'What can I do?' he said. 'You don't know—' The question was not an appeal; it was as simply stated as the 'What good would I be?' when Sam had urged him to enlist.

'Sam, you don't know,' he said. 'God knows, I—' Then he seemed to take a hold on himself. He straightened up wearily, and shrugged again.

'I'm going to tell Bunyard,' Sam said, a great, choking rage welling up in his throat. He let go of the leeboard and

picked up the sculling oar as the rowing-boat dropped away
from *Trilby's* side. Gil leaned on the shroud, watching him
go, but did not call after him. Sam waited for him to call,
but he did not move, nor make any sign.

'He is so ashamed,' Sam thought, 'he is past caring
whether he gets shot for a spy or not.' Bunyard was already
asleep when he got back to the *Flower*. Albert was waiting
in his bunk to hear what Sam had to say.

'You'll tell Bunyard then?' he asked Sam, after hearing
the report.

'Yes, I'll tell him,' Sam said heavily.

Of all the things he had ever had to pluck up his courage
for, to face Bunyard with, there had never been anything
like this. Sam slept, exhausted, through the hot afternoon.
Bunyard woke them in the evening, to get the *Flower*
moved on to the wharf for loading. *Trilby* had moved off
and lay on the buoys, waiting for the tide to start her
journey. Getting off the hatch-covers, Sam saw the work
stretching ahead; in June they loaded until the light failed.
Trilby would be away at midnight. Bunyard had gone
ashore to get his clearances.

'Aren't you going to tell him?' Albert asked.

'I can't if he's not here, can I?' Sam said crossly.

By the time Bunyard returned, *Trilby* had already sailed,
making use of a fresh westerly to stem the flood. Sam, with
a weight inside him like the cargo that was now pressing the
Flower down towards her marks, trailed after Bunyard down
the companion-way steps. He had no feelings left.

'Mr. Bunyard.'

'What do you want?'

'My brother on *Trilby* is carrying messages for the—'
He hesitated.

'For what? Who?'

'You know,' Sam whispered.

Bunyard did not say anything. He looked at Sam thoughtfully, tapping his clearance forms with one hand on to the palm of the other. He nodded.

'That's what's been on your mind then? You're sure what you're saying is true?'

'Yes, I'm sure. He has admitted it.'

'He knows you know?' Bunyard was surprised.

'Yes, he knows, and he knows I'm going to tell you. I told him I was. He says he can't get out of it. I told him to stop, and he doesn't do anything. He just goes on, with that Finch. Finch started him. Finch is the worst, he started him. And Gil's so weak, he can't get out of it.'

'You don't know what he's up against, Sam,' Bunyard said. 'It's not easy to withdraw from a circle of that nature. I've seen some, believe me.' He paused. 'And you're telling me?' he said, curiously. 'You know what you're doing?'

'I've got another brother,' Sam reminded him. 'You don't think I'm telling you on the spur of the moment? You don't think I haven't *thought* about it?' Sam's eyes blazed at Bunyard.

'I told you not to meddle, didn't I?' Bunyard said.

'What else can I do, but tell you? I went to tell Manny, didn't I? And see where that got me? Manny's dying over there, and Gil—well, what could I do?'

'Ah, simmer down,' Bunyard laid his big hand on Sam's shoulder. 'There are ways out of these things, Sam. Gil's only a kid who's got himself in a mess. Finch—he's a different matter perhaps. I told you, you shouldn't meddle, you little fool.' His voice was as gentle as Sam had ever heard it. 'What if I talk to Gil?'

'You talk to him? You mean, it could do any good? I talked to him—he just says, "What can I do?"' Sam stared at Bunyard in an agony of hope. 'You could tell him what to do?'

'If he means well, we could manage something between us, perhaps.'

'He won't be shot?'

'I'll see what I can do.'

'But he's sailed already! When—?'

'We'll catch him before Boulogne, the rate we're being loaded now.' Bunyard was calm, like a rock, in the midst of Sam's quicksand of doubt. Sam felt as if Bunyard were holding him, he a little washed-up, exhausted bit of flotsam. The relief of Bunyard's knowing was inexpressible. Sam just stood, feeling the peace filling him.

'He'll only be a tide ahead of us, if we're lucky,' Bunyard said.

Lucky, Sam thought. Was Manny still lucky?

The *Flower* was loaded by the following midday, and sailed on the top of the tide. The wind was light but fair. The deep-loaded barge thrust up a white bow-wave, heavily running down the river, the nearly two hundred tons of ammunition carefully stacked and wedged in her hold. It was a cleaner cargo than coke, which meant less work for Sam and Albert, and suited them well. The *Flower* made good progress, and was off the Kent coast by evening.

'We must have made up on *Trilby*,' Sam said to Albert, 'because there was scarcely any wind at all this morning. He couldn't have got far.'

'And this wind won't serve once he's round the Foreland,' Albert said. It was a southerly, freshening as dusk came, which kept the *Flower* moving at a good three knots over the tide.

'We'll make Margate by midnight,' Albert said eagerly.

But off Whitstable the wind began to drop light. The *Flower* barely made way. The full moon sailed out of thin cloud and lit the wide path of the estuary like a flare.

'Tide'll be fair again in an hour,' Bunyard said. 'Not worth dropping the hook.'

'This moon, and the wind dropping away—it's an airship night now,' Albert remarked, as a pair of searchlights started to grope over the Kent shore.

'It's not a sailing night, that's for sure,' Bunyard growled. He pulled out his watch and peered at it under the compass light. 'As long as she's making. . . .'

When the tide turned, the *Flower* started to make progress once more, until Sam could make out the spidery arm of Margate pier.

'And look! Topmasts!' he cried out. 'Four, five, six! I bet *Trilby's* one of 'em!'

'The patrol must have pulled 'em up,' Bunyard said. 'They don't like these bright nights. We'll creep in and see if Gil's there. Trust you damned Goodchilds to waste me a fair tide!'

'You'll see him though?' Sam asked anxiously.

'Aye, we'll kick him out of his bunk and find out what the devil he's up to.'

But Gil was on deck as the *Flower of Ipswich* rounded up into the wind. He watched as Albert let go the anchor, and the big barge took up on her chain, sliding heavily to a standstill, winch thrumming as the weight came on it, the chain standing out like a bar with the tide making a white wave on either side. Bunyard came up forward and looked at it despondently.

'Those naval patrol blokes who stop us so blithely—' he spat, viciously, into the tide '—have never got in a barge anchor with a couple of hundred ton weight hanging on it . . .'

They could see the naval patrol boat standing off, making sure that they were anchoring. When the sails were brailed up and her sprit stood out bare against the sky, the patrol boat, satisfied, opened up her throttle and purred away round the North Foreland.

'Ruddy sheep-dogs,' Bunyard said.

' But it's your chance to see Gil,' Sam said anxiously.

' Aye.'

The *Flower* lay downstream, downtide, of *Trilby*. Three barges lay in a line inshore of her, and three more, including *Trilby* were anchored in a line ahead. Inshore, the yards of an old brig stood out, moored against the harbour wall, and the prim house-fronts of Margate rose up whitewashed by the moon, windows glinting, tall chimneys trailing stars. Already in the east, out at sea, dawn was touching the horizon.

They got the rowing-boat launched from its davits, and Bunyard told Sam to go and fetch Gil. ' And if he won't come, tell him his time on earth's up, that's from me. And you'll have to row like hell, with this tide running.'

Sam made the short journey with great difficulty, throwing himself on the oars so that he thought his arms would come out of their sockets. ' And this is the last time, Gil,' he thought. ' I can't do any more, if you don't see sense.'

Gil looked down at him coldly. ' Now what? '

' Bunyard wants to see you.'

' You told him? '

' Yes.'

' It's the police he wants to see then, not me.'

' He said you,' Sam persisted. Gil said nothing. ' For God's sake, I can't sit here all night,' Sam said. Looking up at Gil, he saw *Trilby's* sprit reared against the bright sky, and the searchlights making their restless gavotte from the cliffs of the Foreland.

' Is Finch asleep? '

Gil nodded.

' Come on, then. You've nothing to lose, have you? '

To his great astonishment, Gil then put his legs over the bulwarks and slipped down into the rowing-boat. Scruff followed him with an anxious whine. Sam let go, putting out his oars, speechless with relief. In the moonlight, Gil's face was white and drawn. He looked older than Manny, Sam thought, his eyes drawn back in their sockets, watchful and nervous. His red-gold hair curled over his forehead in the damp air, his cap pushed back. To Sam, he was dangerous, unpredictable, his brother now only by·blood ties, no longer a brother bound by affection. In Gil's face he saw Manny's, sweaty with pain.

He did not have to row back to the *Flower*, only keep the rowing-boat on course and use the oars to stop her fast slide over the tide to go alongside. He thought he heard a whistle shrill on shore. Gil put up a hand and steadied the boat against the *Flower's* side. The barge had little more freeboard than the small boat, and they climbed on board easily, Gil handing up the little dog first. Albert was on deck. He looked at Gil nervously and said, ' Bunyard said go below.' To Sam he said, ' And we can bed down, he said. And about ruddy time too, says I.' He gave an enormous yawn.

' They're getting up over there,' Sam said, trying to be casual, and looking towards the shore. The whistle was still shrilling, and some men were running along the harbour wall. Sam was thinking about Gil, who had already made his way towards the skipper's quarters, Scruff at his heels. He wanted to go too, to hear what Bunyard was going to propose. Albert clutched his arm suddenly.

' You know what's up? ' he said urgently. ' Those whistles—and look at the searchlights dancing around! There must be an airship around.'

' You said it was an airship night! ' Sam said. ' This moon and all. Cor, stone me, I hope it doesn't find this little lot! ' For the first time since he had been doing the munition freight, Sam thought clearly about the nature of the cargo they were standing on.

' Probably going up to London,' Albert said. ' Or on its way home.'

They stood on deck, watching the searchlights. Sam

remembered the airship they had seen when they had anchored off Southend a week ago—it seemed more like a month ago. 'Probably the same one,' he thought. 'Knows his way around now.'

The guns were firing over Chatham and Sheerness. The two boys could hear the thud of the exploding shells and see the bright burst of shell-fire. 'If he's following the river,' Albert said uneasily, 'and he's got any bombs left. . . .'

'He'll have used 'em all by now,' Sam said. 'Can you hear him?'

The thin, distant whine of an unfamiliar engine came on the breeze, and the searchlights began to grope desperately, swooping and circling with the craziness of summer bats. On shore the whistles were shrilling again; somebody was shouting. One by one the barge skippers and crews came up on deck and stood watching, uneasily aware of the cargoes they were standing on, so much more sinister than the grey mountains of coke. Bunyard and Gil came up and stood with Sam and Albert, their business suspended. 'It's queer,' Sam thought, watching Gil out of the corner of his eye, 'this happening now.' Bunyard and Gil were quite easy together, conjecturing about the airship.

'Just as well we anchored,' Albert said to Sam. They could picture the black blob of a sailing barge on the moon-silver sea, seen from above, the great vee of her wake on the calm water. 'He'd have lobbed one on us for sure.'

'Bet you he's used 'em.'

'Well, if he uses any here. . . . !' Albert rolled his eyes.

Sam felt his nerves tingle as the whine of the airship engine came nearer. It was following the line of the coast, he felt sure, although no searchlight had found it yet.

The barges were anchored in two neat tiers, close together in the economical manner of the sailormen, who could judge their place to a nicety. A single stick of bombs might easily find a mark if the Hun pilot were to notice the neat pattern of the sprits.

'He's left it late,' Bunyard growled, nodding over his shoulder. The opal coldness of a summer dawn was putting out the stars behind them, lighting the line of the horizon. Sam remembered the morning when the *Notre Dame de Calais* had shelled them. It was just such a one as this. It cannot happen again, he thought, with that peculiar tightening of the nerves. He was frightened. He could not deny it. The noise of the airship kept on coming, droning like a persistent wasp.

'There!'

They all shouted together, as one of the swooping searchlights caught the squat silver intruder in its beam. It was low and apparently losing gas, and to Sam it looked enormous, ten times longer than a barge, and, with its silvery skin shimmering in the light, unearthly . . . obscene.

Almost immediately the guns opened up. Erratic shell-fire burst over the Margate sea front, lighting up the white stucco, rattling the boarding-house windows.

'If they hit her,' Albert said, 'she'll make a landfall aboard, I reckon.'

'Keep your fingers crossed,' Sam muttered. He was praying for the monster to pass. Lumbering, shining in the searchlight beams, she seemed to hang like a great lantern over the barges. A shell burst very close to her. Sam blinked. He saw the fierce, firework flowering of the explosion, and simultaneously heard the whine of the bombs released. Somebody gave him a fierce shove from behind. 'This is it!' he thought, with the panic bursting, catching his throat, the crescendoing whistle of the bombs filling his ears.

They all flung themselves on the deck. Sam put his arms over his head, to shut out the mounting whistle, felt Albert's frantic boot clobber him on the side of the head. . . .

The *Flower* rocked, as if in a big steamer's wash. There was a crash and a splintering noise, but distant, nothing to do with the barge. She rocked again, confused. Somebody started shouting across the water. Sam, still alive, lifted his head.

' Is that all? ' Albert was saying, close by his ear. The guns were pounding after the Zeppelin, the shells bursting overhead and the casings coming down with vicious small thuds and whistles. They all got to their feet, and looked round. Everything was flooded suddenly with an unearthly red glow, and the air was filled with a roaring noise. It was a more terrifying noise even than the whistle of the bombs.

' The Zep's on fire! ' Albert shouted.

Bunyard said, very matter-of-factly, ' So is *Trilby*.'

Everything was as bright as day, pin-sharp in the lurid light. Crowds lined the Margate sea front, faces studded the flaming window-panes. The Zeppelin hung motionless, roaring, great torches of flaming petrol spouting from its belly. It drifted over the pier, turning every pane of glass to a burning diamond, spouting its flaring fuel into the flat, cold maw of the dawn sea. The white hissing as the two elements joined could be heard even above the roar of the burning gas. Sam saw a little spidery man fall, over and over, arms and legs, into the steaming sea.

' God Almighty! ' Albert said softly.

Gil was standing close by Sam, and Sam found that he was holding Gil's arm. Gil was looking at *Trilby*. He put Sam's arm away, gently, and said, ' Look, I must go to *Trilby*. Keep the dog, Sam. Hold him. Don't let him follow me.'

' Gil, don't go! '

Trilby had been hit by the stern. Her own rowing-boat had been torn from its davits and hung in splinters, and her mizzen-mast was on fire, the flames tearing at her furled canvas. Finch and Scotty were on deck. Scotty was frantically drawing bucketfuls of water to throw over the mizzen, but Finch seemed to be stumbling about in a panic, shouting.

' Drunk,' Albert said. ' God help Gil and Scotty.'

Gil was already in the rowing-boat, putting out the oars. Sam had his arms round the frantic little dog, clutching handfuls of shaggy hair in an effort to hold him as he whined and struggled, seeing Gil leaving him.

' Get that ruddy fire out,' Bunyard shouted at Gil, throwing the painter down into the boat, ' else the whole of Margate will be blown to Kingdom Come. And us with it! '

Gil started rowing, throwing himself on the oars. Sam got a stranglehold on the demented dog and took it forward to the fo'c'sle, slamming the hatch shut on it. Bunyard and Albert came with him, following Gil, their eyes on *Trilby*. All the barge skippers were watching *Trilby* now, in spite of the continuing spectacle of the blazing airship behind them. The unearthly red light showed up every detail of the action on board *Trilby*; it outlined Gil's powerful rowing, and turned his phosphorescent wake blood-red behind him.

' That fire's got a hold,' Bunyard growled. ' They'll be lucky if they check it now.'

Albert was swearing. Sam felt his stomach turn to lead, the fear and the excitement settle, turning him cold.

' What'll happen? ' he said, in a thin voice.

' Just use a bit of imagination, lad,' Bunyard said. ' And then pray to God a miracle will stop it.' He was fingering the anchor-winch. Sam guessed that he had half a mind to let their anchor slip and go, run clear. He stood by the winch, drumming his fingers against his thigh, more moved than Sam had ever seen him.

Gil had reached *Trilby* and had put the boat alongside with a last strong thrust of the oars. He threw the painter up to Finch and scrambled out on deck. Sam heard Scotty shout to him, ' It's no good. It's away like hell.'

' He's right there,' Bunyard muttered.

Finch had obviously been waiting for Gil merely to make use of the rowing-boat to get away in. He was already in it, shouting to Gil and Scotty to hurry, and was about to cast off the painter. But Gil had got hold of the painter and was holding it fast, arguing, swearing at him. Scotty stood, one foot on the bulwarks, looking from one of them to the other. Gil said something to him sharply, and flung the painter down in disgust. He gave Scotty a shove and Scotty half-fell, half-jumped into the rowing-boat that the tide was already plucking away. Gil, without any hesitation, went forward to the mast and picked up the winch-handle. Bunyard smote his thigh with a great chuckle of satisfaction.

'Thank God one of 'em's got a bit of sense in his head! That swine Finch—'

'Gil's going to sail her out!' Sam said wonderingly, as *Trilby's* mainsail started to drop down from its brails. 'But Finch is skipper! It's Finch's job—' He was sharply, horribly afraid for Gil.

'Gil'll make a better job of it than that drunken lout,' Bunyard said.

'He'll need to be ruddy clever to miss us,' Albert said.

'You're right there,' Bunyard said.

Gil was wasting no time, hooking the mainsheet block on to the traveller and hauling in the sheet. *Trilby* snubbed, juddering, on her anchor and the big sprit shook as the wind rattled down the sail. The flames at the mizzen, fed by the passage of the breeze off the filling mainsail, roared up and danced over the transom. Gil was at the wheel, putting the helm over, hauling impatiently on the spokes until the barge started to swing. Heavily, rolling, the painted transom with her canopy of flames slid across the water in answer to the rudder. The anchor still held her. She snubbed up with a grinding of the big links over the stem, pitching and groaning. Gil locked the wheel and ran forward.

'Let her go, lad!' Bunyard muttered. 'Slip the lot! Stand by to fend off, boys. God, she'll go up like the last trump when she goes!'

The chain started to run. They heard the vicious rattle of the links flying, and saw *Trilby* dropping down on them, still swinging, slewing on the tide. Her sail was filled, her bows freed at last, the cast on the rudder slowly turning her. She dropped towards the *Flower*, the plume of flame at her stern like some fantastic, living ensign, leaping to the quickening breeze. Gil had gone back to the wheel to straighten her up, but now the breeze was sweeping the fire forward. As he hauled again on the spokes, the flames reached for him; the burning mizzen sprit broke off half-way up and swung round with a trail of sparks like a Catherine-wheel. Gil ducked. The spar came down with a whoosh of flame, for a moment obliterating Gil in a great fountain of flying sparks and smoke. *Trilby's* bowsprit was twenty feet off the *Flower's* bows, but she was answering her helm, sailing, sliding on the tide, ponderously moving her two hundred tons to the frantic pressure on her rudder. Bunyard, Sam and Albert stood in complete silence as she bore down on them. They heard the creaking of her great sprit, saw the easy turn of her bow-wave. She was picking up way, her sail hardening, and she was still turning, showing her starboard bow. Her bowsprit went past with six feet to spare, and Gil was straightening her up to keep his flaming stern clear. Sam felt the hot draught of the flames on his own face, saw Gil holding the wheel steady, watching the *Flower*. Gil was framed in flames. To Sam, hypnotized with horror, he was the Devil in hell, the flames wreathing him, his clothes smouldering, his features contorted with pain almost out of recognition. The flames were creeping along the deck; the mizzen was consumed, fallen in a tangle of charred, smoking debris, steaming brands dropping in her glowing wake. For the last time Gil put down his helm. *Trilby* had cleared the *Flower*, now she turned in a broad reach out away from the shore. She gathered way, and Gil put the lock on the wheel and went forward at last. Sam saw him stagger, beating at his smoking trouser-legs. He went to the mast and leaned on it, holding his face in his hands.

'Good lad,' Bunyard said quietly. He put the winch-handle down and stood, heavily, watching.

'How's he going to get off?' Albert said. 'The rowing-boat's in splinters.'

Sam had nothing to say. He felt as if the world had stopped being real. The sea was bathed in the volcanic light of the dying Zeppelin: *Trilby* and the pier and the sea front and the whole population of Margate, flame-faced and awed. 'Never,' Sam thought, 'will anything like this happen to me again. And it hasn't finished yet. There's *Trilby* to blow up.'

'How's he going to get off?' Albert said again.

All the barge crews were watching *Trilby*, standing in grave knots on deck. The naval patrol boat was coming back, a distant, gilded speck against the spreading dawn, but Bunyard said bitterly, 'They'll steer well clear of *Trilby*, you watch. They know what she's carrying.' A fleet of rowing-boats had gone out from the shore, and hovered at a safe distance round the burning airship, but one rowing-boat was trailing *Trilby*. Its occupant could not keep up with her but he followed, a man rowing alone.

'It's Scotty,' Albert said.

'Finch has left him to it,' Bunyard said. 'Trust him.'

The airship had hit the sea, and was collapsing in a hissing cauldron of steam. It was as if the steam itself consumed the great carcass, writhing up the ribs of blackened aluminium, pouncing on the charred tatters of cloth, obliterating the terrifying flame. Dense clouds poured upwards and hung on the soft breeze, at first reddened by the flame below like a sunset, and then, as the flames died, softening and dispersing, touched merely by the pearly light of the dawn sky. Sam looked up and saw that the stars had gone. The sky was luminous with the coming sun. It was cold, very clear, the sea very calm.

In the light wind *Trilby* was not travelling fast, but as they watched her, the big black triangle of her foresail started to go up on the stay. The barge skippers watched in silence. It flogged lazily, and was sheeted home, and started to draw. Then the topsail was broken loose and hauled out.

'Good God,' Albert said. 'Anyone'd think he's going to Boulogne.'

'Everything,' Bunyard said. 'Set everything. That's my boy. Do it in style.' He spoke softly, his voice full of admiration.

Now *Trilby* was moving. A white lip curled from her stem; the sparks danced over her wheel, and the flames ate along her deck. Her mizzen trailed burning debris, her skylight was spouting thick white smoke which the wind lifted and spun, flame-shot, into the sky. But the jib was set on her raking bowsprit, and the white jib topsail stood out sharp against the sky like a gull's wing. Her wake lengthened, hurrying, and the flames, fanned by her haste, started to leap up from the deck, reaching for the great red mainsail. The smoke poured up from her coamings. Well out to sea now, it was as if the barge herself were defying the fire, lifting her sails to the sky as if she would take to flight. The flames leapt, and the first tongue caught the mainsail.

A great sigh went up from the watching crowds. The flames raced up the sail, making a wall of fire, which lasted for mere seconds. The topsail flared, a great orange burst of flame, then the canvas started to drop away in ragged burning gouts. But even as the barge faltered, Bunyard said, 'She'll go out sailing. She will.'

Behind the smoking sprit the tip of a red sun was just showing above the horizon. With all her foresails still pulling *Trilby* was running off before the wind, unbalanced by the loss of her main. She was making for the sun, romping for home, carrying her wild fire like a banner. Sam saw her bowsprit cross the red ball of the sun . . . then something

seemed to punch him in the chest, plucking all the breath out of his body. He gasped, blinked. When he opened his eyes, *Trilby* was no longer there.

The noise of the explosion was almost a physical pain, slamming the eardrums. Sam looked blindly at Bunyard, and saw his lips moving, but could hear no words. Bunyard reached out an arm to Sam, and Sam went to him like a child.

'Trust you Goodchilds,' Bunyard was saying, his hand on Sam's shoulder. 'Trust you to make a good job of it.' He was smiling with what Sam could only think of as pride.

The wash of the explosion came suddenly, and the two tiers of barges rolled like dinghies, clattering gear. Down in the fo'c'sle, Sam heard the little dog start to howl.

10 The Letter for Gil

Sam went home again. The naval patrol boat took him to
Southend, and he stood on her deck and watched the little
fleet of barges make sail on the tail of the ebb. This time, he
would have given every penny he possessed to be going
with them, out into the glittering sea off the Foreland. He
shrank from going home. Every noisy mile churned out by
the screw of the naval launch pitched his misery a notch
lower. He stood hunched-up, white-faced, staring at the
smooth sea where *Trilby* had been, where the patrol boat
had circled for half an hour before coming to report to the
silent fleet of barges.

'Matchwood, it's all matchwood,' they had said.

'And the boy?'

They had shrugged. 'He won't need a funeral.'

All Sam could think of now was Manny. He prayed
furiously, over and over in his head, for Manny to keep on
living. He got on the train, and stared out of the window,

saying, over and over, 'Keep lucky, Manny. For God's sake, keep lucky.' For Gil, there was a great blankness. Scotty had come back, crying, ashamed of having left him. They had let the little dog out, and he had gone, howling, to Scotty. Scotty had sailed on the *Flower*. Finch had disappeared ashore, but Bunyard had promised Sam that Finch would get what was coming to him. 'I'll see the Guv'nor. He'll fix him.' Finch, as yet, had no reason to believe that he was suspected of anything worse than cowardice.

Sam changed trains. The train left Wickford, and steamed serenely down the valley of the infant Crouch, past the Battlesbridge mills, where Gil had first met Finch—less than a year ago; Gil had been easy and laughing, and cycling to meet Agnes—down through the hayfields to Woodham, where the pea trains were shunting about and a cartload of pigs was held up at the crossing. On the river, when the train rolled on, skirting the marshes, Sam saw barge sails. He saw the woods of Fambridge running down to meet the river, and he had to force himself to get out when the train stopped, to overcome the impulse to go on to Burnham and get himself drunk. Even so, he could not go home. He walked down to the ' Ferry-Boat ' and got himself a rum.

' Go and tell my mother Gil is dead,' he said to the barmaid, who had once walked out with Manny.

He drank the rum, and then another, and felt easier, as if he were floating over this great sea of trouble, instead of drowning in it. Everyone was coming and going. There was a soldier at his house, they told him, calling on his mother.

' But Manny is—is—'

' It's not Manny. It's a mate of his.'

' What's he called for? '

' He says Manny's wounded, but all right. He called to tell her.'

Sam went home to see the soldier. The house was full of women talking, and the soldier was backing out, anxious to take his leave. Sam recognized him as a shipwright from Burnham, who had volunteered with Manny. He looked shaken.

'I come to tell 'er about Manny, and then this damned woman comes weeping in the door saying Gil's copped it, and there I was with 'em all. Mate, I want a drink.'

'You're sure about Manny?' Sam asked him.

'I saw him last night. They've moved him to Boulogne. He's tough as old boots, Manny. He stopped a packet all right, but he'll come through. I got leave, and I knew they shifted him into hospital, so I stopped off and had a look at him before the ship sailed. I tell you, he'll come through all right. It's rough about Gil, though.'

'As long as Manny's all right,' Sam said stubbornly.

Fortified by his floating feeling, he went into the house. The women were all talking about the funeral. 'There won't be no funeral,' Sam said to them. 'How can you have a funeral when—' His mother seemed to have shrunk still further into her little, hard black-beetle shell.

'Is it true about Gil, Sam? You're sure?'

'Oh, yes, I'm sure all right. I saw it.'

'We heard it,' one of the women said eagerly. 'It woke us up, the explosion. My husband said it was in the Thames. We thought—'

'Yes, I heard it too.'

'Lot of vultures,' Sam thought. On the mantelshelf, tucked behind a vase, there was a little buff official envelope, addressed to Gil.

'What's this?' he asked his mother.

'I don't know. It came a couple of days ago.'

'I'd better open it.'

He stood in front of the fire, and examined the letter. He shook out the single leaf of paper, and read it carefully. It said:

'You, Gilbert Arthur Goodchild, are required to attend at

9 o'clock on the fourteenth day of July at Colchester
Barracks for the purpose of . . .'

He read it several times, and the floating feeling left him,
abruptly.

'What is it?' his mother asked.

'He'd enlisted. It's his calling-up papers. To report to
Colchester.' Sam could not believe it. He kept reading the
letter over and over again. 'He'd volunteered.'

'Throw it in the fire.'

But Sam was hypnotized by it. He smoothed it out,
stroking the buff paper. 'He'd volunteered. He never said.'

'He never said much.'

Sam was groping for Gil's motive. Had it been a gesture
of despair, to escape from his troubles? To impress Agnes?
To get right with his conscience? But why . . . ? Would
he have told Bunyard, if he had not been interrupted? Sam
knew that he would never know. Only the great blankness
that he felt for Gil dissolved. God only knew, Gil had atoned,
and shown as much courage at his end as any Mons veteran;
even if he had been saved, he would have been dreadfully
burned. Sam shuddered, remembering Gil's face. He clutched
the scrap of paper with a desperate desire for the floating
feeling to come back and save him, to insulate him again
from reality. He backed out of the house and went back to
the ' Ferry-Boat ', to find Manny's friend.

'Manny'll be home when he's healed up a bit,' the
soldier said.

Sam's face brightened. 'For quite a bit, probably?'

'He won't go back in a hurry,' the soldier agreed.

Sam visualized his mother nursing Manny. All the weeks
of the summer, and into the autumn she would have Manny
to look after. His hand curled round the letter in his pocket.

'What's it like, over there?' he asked.

'Nobody wants to know, at home,' the soldier said. 'You
tell 'em a bit, and they don't believe you. You can't tell 'em

really. If they don't believe just the little bit you tell 'em, what's the good of telling them all of it?' He had drunk several pints of beer, and stared happily into the distance.

'You want to go back?'

'No, I don't want to go back. But they make you sick at home. All making a fortune, and being patriotic. Almost makes you glad to get shot of 'em, 'n go back again. It's more real back there.'

Sam fingered the letter again. His mother had plenty of company now, and in a week or two she would have Manny. He went home, and slept the clock round, and left the house early, before his mother was up. He walked to the station and got on a train.

He went to Colchester and walked out to the barracks. As he got near the gate, several men passed him, rather diffident like himself, pulling their ties straight, whistling nervously. Sam rubbed his shoes on the backs of his trouser legs and smoothed his hair under his cap. He had no luggage grip, like most of the recruits, nor even his barge kit-bag. Only the letter. His fingers were sticky on the letter in his pocket. He straightened up and went to the gate. The sentry only gave him a glance, and jerked his head inside the gate.

'Report to the guard-room.'

The guard-room was full of excited, nervous recruits, waiting to show their papers to the sergeant who stood behind a scrubbed table, moustache bristling. Sam had to wait, and while he waited the nervousness rose up inside him, drying his throat, twitching his lips. All the other men looked old, he thought: one man had a lined, grandfather's face round his clear, excited eyes. 'They're all nervous,' Sam thought, fidgetting with his letter. He glanced at the clock. Sunlight streamed in through the polished windows and Sam had a sudden vision of the *Flower of Ipswich* sailing down to Boulogne past Gris Nez, the gulls wheeling over the great chalk downs and the faraway guns rolling like distant thunder in the sky. All three of them, Manny, Gil and himself, could have been sailing now, had they but chosen: the sea calm and fair, the birds crying over the sprits and the wakes drawing out white and straight. Sun on your face, and shirt-sleeves, Sam thought, like a Bank holiday outing. But Manny and Gil were out of it, and he . . . he clutched the letter and prayed. The man in front of him was next at the scrubbed table, handing over his papers. Someone said to Sam, curiously, ' You eighteen, then? '

' Yes,' said Sam.

The sergeant barked at him. ' You! '

Sam handed up his letter, and licked his lips.

' Gilbert Arthur Goodchild.' The sergeant stared at Sam.

' Yes, sir.'

' I don't know what the army's coming to, taking on shrimps like you. What's your age? '

' Eighteen, sir.'

' You showed your birth certificate? '

' Yes, sir.'

The sergeant peered at Sam again, suspiciously, and back at the letter. Everything was in order. He sighed.

' Hop along then. Down the passage.'

Sam's heart swooped. He beamed.

' Yes, sir! '

He went out of the room, under the clock. The *Flower of Ipswich* would be going into Boulogne now. ' I'll make it right with Mr. Bunyard,' Sam thought. He gave a little skip. Then, remembering his age, he turned it into a military swagger, and strode away down the passage.

Glossary

BINNACLE   Receptacle for ship's compass.

BOB   Flag.

BOWSPRIT   Spar running outboard from the bows.

BRAILS   Ropes which gather up the mainsail when reefing or bringing up. On a barge there are three, known as mains, middles and lowers.

COAMING   Raised boards round hatches to keep out the water.

DAVIT   Hoist for raising and lowering the barge's small boat. The boat hangs in it when the barge is under way.

GYBE   When the mainsail swings across from one side to the other with the wind behind it. This can be done inadvertently if the boat is running before the wind and the helmsman is careless. It can then be very dangerous, in strong winds bringing down the mast.

HALYARDS   Ropes for hauling sails up and down.

HORSE   A bar across the deck on which the sheet of a sail may move.

TO LUFF   To bring the barge up into the wind, slowing or stopping her.

MAINSTAY   One of the shrouds.

MIZZEN   Small sail at the stern.

PAINTER   Rope for making a small boat fast to a mooring or another boat.

SHEET   A rope by means of which a sail is trimmed and secured.

SHROUDS   Rope or wire stays that support mast.

TRANSOM   Flat stern of barge.

VANG   A rope controlling the upper end of the sprit.

WARP   A rope used for towing or making fast.

TO WARP   Pull a boat along by a rope.

Other great reads ∕*from* **Red Fox**

Further Red Fox titles that you might enjoy reading are listed
on the following pages. They are available in bookshops or they
can be ordered directly from us.

If you would like to order books, please send this form and
the money due to:

**ARROW BOOKS, BOOKSERVICE BY POST, PO BOX 29,
DOUGLAS, ISLE OF MAN, BRITISH ISLES.** Please enclose
a cheque or postal order made out to Arrow Books Ltd for the
amount due, plus 22p per book for postage and packing, both
for orders within the UK and for overseas orders.

NAME _____

ADDRESS _____

_____

Please print clearly.

Whilst every effort is made to keep prices low, it is sometimes
necessary to increase cover prices at short notice. If you are
ordering books by post, to save delay it is advisable to phone
to confirm the correct price. The number to ring is THE SALES
DEPARTMENT 071 (if outside London) 973 9700.

Other great reads from **Red Fox**

Enter the gripping world of the REDWALL saga

REDWALL   Brian Jacques

It is the start of the summer of the Late Rose. Redwall Abbey, the peaceful home of a community of mice, slumbers in the warmth of a summer afternoon. The mice are preparing for a great jubilee feast.

But not for long. Cluny is coming! The evil one-eyed rat warlord is advancing with his battle-scarred mob. And Cluny wants Redwall . . .

ISBN 0 09 951200 9   £3.50

MOSSFLOWER   Brian Jacques

One late autumn evening, Bella of Brockhall snuggled deep in her armchair and told a story . . .

This is the dramatic tale behind the bestselling *Redwall*. It is the gripping account of how Redwall Abbey was founded through the bravery of the legendary mouse Martin and his epic quest for Salmandastron. Once again, the forces of good and evil are at war in a stunning novel that will captivate readers of all ages.

ISBN 0 09 955400 3   £3.50

MATTIMEO   Brian Jacques

Slagar the fox is intent on revenge . . .

On bringing death and destruction to the inhabitants of Redwall Abbey, in particular to the fearless warrior mouse Matthias. Gathering his evil band around him, Slagar plots to strike at the heart of the Abbey. His cunning and cowardly plan is to steal the Redwall children—and Mattimeo, Matthias' son, is to be the biggest prize of all.

ISBN 0 09 967540 4   £3.50

Other great reads from **Red Fox**

THE SNIFF STORIES Ian Whybrow

Things just keep happening to Ben Moore. It's dead hard avoiding disaster when you've got to keep your street cred with your mates *and* cope with a family of oddballs at the same time. There's his appalling 2½ year old sister, his scatty parents who are into healthy eating and animal rights and, worse than all of these, there's Sniff! If only Ben could just get on with his scientific experiments and his attempt at a world beating *Swampbeast* score . . . but there's no chance of that while chaos is just around the corner.

ISBN 0 09 9750406 £2.50

J.B. SUPERSLEUTH Joan Davenport

James Bond is a small thirteen-year-old with spots and spectacles. But with a name like that, how can he help being a supersleuth?

It all started when James and 'Polly' (Paul) Perkins spotted a teacher's stolen car. After that, more and more mysteries needed solving. With the case of the Arabian prince, the Murdered Model, the Bonfire Night Murder and the Lost Umbrella, JB's reputation at Moorside Comprehensive soars.

But some of the cases aren't quite what they seem . . .

ISBN 0 09 9717808 £1.99

Other great reads from **Red Fox**

The Maggie Series   Joan Lingard

MAGGIE 1: THE CLEARANCE

Sixteen-year-old Maggie McKinley's dreading the prospect of
a whole summer with her granny in a remote Scottish glen. But
the holiday begins to look more exciting when Maggie meets
the Frasers. She soon becomes best friends with James and
spends almost all her time with him. Which leads, indirectly,
to a terrible accident . . .

ISBN 0 09 947730 0   £1.99

MAGGIE 2: THE RESETTLING

Maggie McKinley's family has been forced to move to a high
rise flat and her mother is on the verge of a nervous breakdown.
As her family begins to rely more heavily on her, Maggie finds
less and less time for her schoolwork and her boyfriend James.
The pressures mount and Maggie slowly realizes that she alone
must control the direction of her life.

ISBN 0 09 949220 2   £1.99

MAGGIE 3: THE PILGRIMAGE

Maggie is now seventeen. Though a Glaswegian through and
through, she is very much looking forward to a cycling holiday
with her boyfriend James. But James begins to annoy Maggie
and tensions mount. Then they meet two Canadian boys and
Maggie finds she is strongly attracted to one of them.

ISBN 0 09 951190 8   £2.50

MAGGIE 4: THE REUNION

At eighteen, Maggie McKinley has been accepted for university
and is preparing to face the world. On her first trip abroad, she
flies to Canada to a summer au pair job and a reunion with Phil,
the Canadian student she met the previous summer. But as usual
in Maggie's life, events don't go quite as planned . . .

ISBN 0 09 951260 2   £2.50

Other great reads *from Red Fox*

THE WINTER VISITOR   Joan Lingard

Strangers didn't come to Nick Murray's home town in winter.
And they didn't lodge at his house. But Ed Black had—and Nick
Murray didn't like it.

   Why had Ed come? The small Scottish seaside resort was
bleak, cold and grey at that time of year. The answer, Nick
begins to suspect, lies with his mother—was there some past
connection between her and Ed?

ISBN 0 09 938590 2   £1.99

STRANGERS IN THE HOUSE   Joan Lingard

Calum resents his mother remarrying. He doesn't want to move
to a flat in Edinburgh with a new father and a thirteen-year-old
stepsister. Stella, too, dreads the new marriage. Used to living
alone with her father she loathes the idea of sharing their small
flat.

   Stella's and Calum's struggles to adapt to a new life, while
trying to cope with the problems of growing up are related with
great poignancy in a book which will be enjoyed by all older
readers.

ISBN 0 09 955020 2   £1.95

Other great reads from Red Fox

Discover the great animal stories of Colin Dann

JUST NUFFIN

The Summer holidays loomed ahead with nothing to look forward to except one dreary week in a caravan with only Mum and Dad for company. Roger was sure he'd be bored.

But then Dad finds Nuffin: an abandoned puppy who's more a bundle of skin and bones than a dog. Roger's holiday is transformed and he and Nuffin are inseparable. But Dad is adamant that Nuffin must find a new home. Is there *any* way Roger can persuade him to change his mind?

ISBN 0 09 966900 5   £1.99

KING OF THE VAGABONDS

'You're very young,' Sammy's mother said, 'so heed my advice. Don't go into Quartermile Field.'

His mother and sister are happily domesticated but Sammy, the tabby cat, feels different. They are content with their lot, never wondering what lies beyond their immediate surroundings. But Sammy is burningly curious and his life seems full of mysteries. Who is his father? Where has he gone? And what is the mystery of Quartermile Field?

ISBN 0 09 957190 0   £2.50

Other great reads *from* **Red Fox**

**The Millennium books are novels for older
readers from the very best science fiction and
fantasy writers**

A DARK TRAVELLING   Roger Zelazny

An 'ordinary' 14-year-old, James Wiley has lost his father to
a parallel world in the darkbands. With the help of his sister
Becky, James, the exchange student and Uncle George, the
werewolf, James goes in search of his parent.

ISBN 0 09 960970 3   £2.99

PROJECT PENDULUM   Robert Silverberg

Identical twins Sean and Eric have been chosen for a daring
experiment. One of them will travel into the distant past. The
other into the distant future. And with each swing of the time
pendulum they will be further apart . . .

ISBN 0 09 962460 5   £2.99

THE LEGACY OF LEHR   Katherine Kurtz

The interstellar cruiser *Valkyrie* is forced to pick up four sinister,
exotic cats, much to the captain's misgivings. His doubts appear
justified when a spate of vicious murders appear on board.

ISBN 0 09 960960 6   £2.99

CHESS WITH A DRAGON   David Gerrold

The Galactic InterChange was the greatest discovery in history
. . . but now it had brought disaster. Unless Yake could
negotiate a deal with the alien in front of him, mankind would
be reduced to a race of slaves.

ISBN 0 09 960950 9   £2.99

Other great reads ⌐*from Red Fox*

Fantasy fiction—the Song of the Lioness series

ALANNA—THE FIRST ADVENTURE
Tamora Pierce

Alanna has just one wish—to become a knight. Her twin brother, Thom, prefers magic and wants to be a great sorcerer. So they swop places and Alanna, dressed as a boy, sets off for the king's court. Becoming a knight is difficult—but Alanna is brave and determined to succeed. And her gift for magic is to prove essential to her survival . . .

ISBN 0 09 943560 8   £2.50

IN THE HAND OF THE GODDESS
Tamora Pierce

Alan of Trebond is the smallest but toughest of the squires at court. Only Prince Jonathan knows she is really a girl called Alanna.

As she prepares for her final training to become a knight, Alanna is troubled. Is she the only one to sense the evil in Duke Roger? Does no one realise what a threat his steely ambition poses?

Alanna must use every ounce of her warrior skills and her gift for magic if she is to survive her Ordeal of Knighthood—and outwit the dangerous sorcerer duke.

ISBN 0 09 955560 3   £2.50

The third title in the Song of the Lioness series, THE GIRL WHO RIDES LIKE A MAN will be published by Red Fox in May 1991.

Other great reads **from Red Fox**

Haunting fiction for older readers from Red Fox

THE XANADU MANUSCRIPT
John Rowe Townsend

There is nothing unusual about visitors in Cambridge.

So what is it about three tall strangers which fills John with a mixture of curiosity and unease? Not only are they strikingly handsome but, for apparently educated people, they are oddly surprised and excited by normal, everyday events. And, as John pursues them, their mystery only seems to deepen.

Set against a background of an old university town, this powerfully compelling story is both utterly fantastic and oddly convincing.

'An author from whom much is expected and received.' *Economist*

ISBN 0 09 9751801 £2.50

ONLOOKER   Roger Davenport

Peter has always enjoyed being in Culver Wood, and dismissed the tales of hauntings, witchcraft and superstitions associated with it. But when he starts having extraordinary visions that are somehow connected with the wood, and which become more real to him than his everyday life, he realizes that something is taking control of his mind in an inexplicable and frightening way.

Through his uneasy relationship with Isobel and her father, a Professor of Archaeology interested in excavating Culver Wood, Peter is led to the discovery of the wood's secret and his own terrifying part in it.

ISBN 0 09 9750708 £2.50

Other great reads *from* **Red Fox**

AMAZING ORIGAMI FOR CHILDREN
Steve and Megumi Biddle

Origami is an exciting and easy way to make toys, decorations and all kinds of useful things from folded paper.

Use leftover gift paper to make a party hat and a fancy box. Or create a colourful lorry, a pretty rose and a zoo full of origami animals. There are over 50 fun projects in Amazing Origami.

Following Steve and Megumi's step-by-step instructions and clear drawings, you'll amaze your friends and family with your magical paper creations.

ISBN 0 09 9661802   £4.99

MAGICAL STRING   Steve and Megumi Biddle

With only a loop of string you can make all kinds of shapes, puzzles and games. Steve and Megumi Biddle provide all the instructions and diagrams that are needed to create their amazing string magic in another of their inventive and absorbing books.

ISBN 0 09 964470 3   £2.50